"There is nothing like Richard Brautigan anywhere. Perhaps, when we are very old, people will write 'Brautigans,' just as we now write novels. This man has invented a genre, a whole new shot, a thing needed, delightful, and right."

— *San Francisco Sunday Examiner & Chronicle*

"*Trout Fishing in America* taps a central metaphor of American literature and deserves to survive the time in which it was written."

— Peter S. Prescott *Newsweek*

"This is an important publication. These books are fun to read. By opening yourself to them, you can get all the old fictional good things. Right there in your own imaginable home you can laugh, tingle, cry and admire. And much of the style lies in Brautigan's speed of delivery."

— Thomas McGuane *New York Times Book Review*

Books by Richard Brautigan

NOVELS

Trout Fishing in America
A Confederate General from Big Sur
In Watermelon Sugar
The Abortion: An Historical Romance 1966
The Hawkline Monster: A Gothic Western
Willard and His Bowling Trophies: A Perverse Mystery
Sombrero Fallout: A Japanese Novel
Dreaming of Babylon: A Private Eye Novel 1942
The Tokyo-Montana Express
So the Wind Won't Blow It All Away

POETRY

The Galilee Hitch-Hiker
Lay the Marble Tea
The Octopus Frontier
All Watched Over by Machines of Loving Grace
Please Plant This Book
The Pill *versus* the Springhill Mine Disaster
Rommel Drives on Deep into Egypt
Loading Mercury with a Pitchfork
June 30th, June 30th

SHORT STORIES

Revenge of the Lawn

Richard Brautigan's

Trout Fishing in America,
The Pill *versus*
the Springhill Mine Disaster,
and
In Watermelon Sugar

(Three books in the manner of their original editions.)

Houghton Mifflin/Seymour Lawrence

BOSTON

For information about permission to reproduce selections
from this book, write to Permissions, Houghton Mifflin
Company, 2 Park Street, Boston, Massachusetts 02108.

Library of Congress Cataloging-in-Publication Data

Brautigan, Richard.
[Selections.   1989]
Richard Brautigan's Trout fishing in America;
The pill versus the Springhill mine disaster;
and, In watermelon sugar.
p.   cm.
ISBN 0-395-50076-1
ISBN 978-0-395-50076-7

I. Title.   II. Title: Trout fishing in America.
III. Title: Pill versus the Springhill mine disaster.
IV. Title: In watermelon sugar.
PS3503.R2736A6   1989
813'.54 — dc19   88-38993
CIP

Printed in the United States of America

DOC 40 39 38 37 36 35

Cover photograph by Erik Weber
Other photographs by Edmund Shea

Writing 14

I N

G   A

N   M

I   E

H   R

S   I

I   C

F   A

T

R   a novel by

O

U   RICHARD BRAUTIGAN

T

For Jack Spicer and Ron Loewinsohn

CONTENTS

There are seductions that should be

in the Smithsonian Institute,

right next to The Spirit of St. Louis.

Trout Fishing in America

THE COVER FOR

TROUT FISHING IN AMERICA

The cover for <u>Trout Fishing in America</u> is a photograph taken late in the afternoon, a photograph of the Benjamin Franklin statue in San Francisco's Washington Square.

Born 1706—Died 1790, Benjamin Franklin stands on a pedestal that looks like a house containing stone furniture. He holds some papers in one hand and his hat in the other.

Then the statue speaks, saying in marble:

PRESENTED BY

H. D. COGSWELL

TO OUR

BOYS AND GIRLS

WHO WILL SOON

TAKE OUR PLACES

AND PASS ON.

Around the base of the statue are four words facing the directions of this world, to the east WELCOME, to the west WELCOME, to the north WELCOME, to the south WELCOME. Just behind the statue are three poplar trees, almost leafless except for the top branches. The statue stands in front of the middle tree. All around the grass is wet from the rains of early February.

1

In the background is a tall cypress tree, almost dark like a room. Adlai Stevenson spoke under the tree in 1956, before a crowd of 40,000 people.

There is a tall church across the street from the statue with crosses, steeples, bells and a vast door that looks like a huge mousehole, perhaps from a Tom and Jerry cartoon, and written above the door is "Per L'Universo."

Around five o'clock in the afternoon of my cover for Trout Fishing in America, people gather in the park across the street from the church and they are hungry.

It's sandwich time for the poor.

But they cannot cross the street until the signal is given. Then they all run across the street to the church and get their sandwiches that are wrapped in newspaper. They go back to the park and unwrap the newspaper and see what their sandwiches are all about.

A friend of mine unwrapped his sandwich one afternoon and looked inside to find just a leaf of spinach. That was all.

Was it Kafka who learned about America by reading the autobiography of Benjamin Franklin . . .

Kafka who said, "I like the Americans because they are healthy and optimistic."

KNOCK ON WOOD

(PART ONE)

As a child when did I first hear about trout fishing in America?
From whom? I guess it was a stepfather of mine.

Summer of 1942.

The old drunk told me about trout fishing. When he could
talk, he had a way of describing trout as if they were a precious
and intelligent metal.

Silver is not a good adjective to describe what I felt when
he told me about trout fishing.

I'd like to get it right.

Maybe trout steel. Steel made from trout. The clear
snow-filled river acting as foundry and heat.

Imagine Pittsburgh.

A steel that comes from trout, used to make buildings,
trains and tunnels.

The Andrew Carnegie of Trout!

The Reply of Trout Fishing in America:

I remember with particular amusement, people with three-
cornered hats fishing in the dawn.

3

KNOCK ON WOOD

(PART TWO)

One spring afternoon as a child in the strange town of Port-
land, I walked down to a different street corner, and saw a
row of old houses, huddled together like seals on a rock.
Then there was a long field that came sloping down off a hill.
The field was covered with green grass and bushes. On top
of the hill there was a grove of tall, dark trees. At a distance
I saw a waterfall come pouring down off the hill. It was long
and white and I could almost feel its cold spray.

There must be a creek there, I thought, and it probably
has trout in it.

Trout.

At last an opportunity to go trout fishing, to catch my first
trout, to behold Pittsburgh.

It was growing dark. I didn't have time to go and look at
the creek. I walked home past the glass whiskers of the
houses, reflecting the downward rushing waterfalls of night.

The next day I would go trout fishing for the first time. I
would get up early and eat my breakfast and go. I had heard
that it was better to go trout fishing early in the morning.
The trout were better for it. They had something extra in
the morning. I went home to prepare for trout fishing in
America. I didn't have any fishing tackle, so I had to fall
back on corny fishing tackle.

Like a joke.

Why did the chicken cross the road?

I bent a pin and tied it onto a piece of white string.

And slept.

The next morning I got up early and ate my breakfast. I
took a slice of white bread to use for bait. I planned on mak-
ing doughballs from the soft center of the bread and putting
them on my vaudevillean hook.

I left the place and walked down to the different street

4

corner. How beautiful the field looked and the creek that
came pouring down in a waterfall off the hill.

But as I got closer to the creek I could see that something
was wrong. The creek did not act right. There was a strange-
ness to it. There was a thing about its motion that was wrong.
Finally I got close enough to see what the trouble was.

The waterfall was just a flight of white wooden stairs
leading up to a house in the trees.

I stood there for a long time, looking up and looking down,
following the stairs with my eyes, having trouble believing.

Then I knocked on my creek and heard the sound of wood.

I ended up by being my own trout and eating the slice of
bread myself.

The Reply of Trout Fishing in America:

There was nothing I could do. I couldn't change a flight of
stairs into a creek. The boy walked back to where he came
from. The same thing once happened to me. I remember
mistaking an old woman for a trout stream in Vermont, and
I had to beg her pardon.

"Excuse me," I said. "I thought you were a trout stream."

"I'm not," she said.

RED LIP

Seventeen years later I sat down on a rock. It was under a tree next to an old abandoned shack that had a sheriff's notice nailed like a funeral wreath to the front door.

NO TRESPASSING

4/17 OF A HAIKU

Many rivers had flowed past those seventeen years, and thousands of trout, and now beside the highway and the sheriff's notice flowed yet another river, the Klamath, and I was trying to get thirty-five miles downstream to Steelhead, the place where I was staying.

It was all very simple. No one would stop and pick me up even though I was carrying fishing tackle. People usually stop and pick up a fisherman. I had to wait three hours for a ride.

The sun was like a huge fifty-cent piece that someone had poured kerosene on and then had lit with a match and said, "Here, hold this while I go get a newspaper," and put the coin in my hand, but never came back.

I had walked for miles and miles until I came to the rock under the tree and sat down. Every time a car would come by, about once every ten minutes, I would get up and stick out my thumb as if it were a bunch of bananas and then sit back down on the rock again.

The old shack had a tin roof colored reddish by years of wear, like a hat worn under the guillotine. A corner of the roof was loose and a hot wind blew down the river and the loose corner clanged in the wind.

A car went by. An old couple. The car almost swerved off

the road and into the river. I guess they didn't see many hitchhikers up there. The car went around the corner with both of them looking back at me.

I had nothing else to do, so I caught salmon flies in my landing net. I made up my own game. It went like this: I couldn't chase after them. I had to let them fly to me. It was something to do with my mind. I caught six.

A little ways up from the shack was an outhouse with its door flung violently open. The inside of the outhouse was exposed like a human face and the outhouse seemed to say, "The old guy who built me crapped in here 9,745 times and he's dead now and I don't want anyone else to touch me. He was a good guy. He built me with loving care. Leave me alone. I'm a monument now to a good ass gone under. There's no mystery here. That's why the door's open. If you have to crap, go in the bushes like the deer."

"Fuck you," I said to the outhouse. "All I want is a ride down the river."

THE KOOL-AID WINO

When I was a child I had a friend who became a Kool-Aid
wino as the result of a rupture. He was a member of a very
large and poor German family. All the older children in the
family had to work in the fields during the summer, picking
beans for two-and-one-half cents a pound to keep the family
going. Everyone worked except my friend who couldn't be-
cause he was ruptured. There was no money for an opera-
tion. There wasn't even enough money to buy him a truss.
So he stayed home and became a Kool-Aid wino.

One morning in August I went over to his house. He was
still in bed. He looked up at me from underneath a tattered
revolution of old blankets. He had never slept under a sheet
in his life.

"Did you bring the nickel you promised?" he asked.

"Yeah," I said. "It's here in my pocket."

"Good."

He hopped out of bed and he was already dressed. He had
told me once that he never took off his clothes when he went
to bed.

"Why bother?" he had said. "You're only going to get up,
anyway. Be prepared for it. You're not fooling anyone by
taking your clothes off when you go to bed."

He went into the kitchen, stepping around the littlest
children, whose wet diapers were in various stages of an-
archy. He made his breakfast: a slice of homemade bread
covered with Karo syrup and peanut butter.

"Let's go," he said.

We left the house with him still eating the sandwich. The
store was three blocks away, on the other side of a field
covered with heavy yellow grass. There were many pheas-
ants in the field. Fat with summer they barely flew away
when we came up to them.

8

"Hello," said the grocer. He was bald with a red birthmark on his head. The birthmark looked just like an old car parked on his head. He automatically reached for a package of grape Kool-Aid and put it on the counter.

"Five cents."

"He's got it," my friend said.

I reached into my pocket and gave the nickel to the grocer. He nodded and the old red car wobbled back and forth on the road as if the driver were having an epileptic seizure.

We left.

My friend led the way across the field. One of the pheasants didn't even bother to fly. He ran across the field in front of us like a feathered pig.

When we got back to my friend's house the ceremony began. To him the making of Kool-Aid was a romance and a ceremony. It had to be performed in an exact manner and with dignity.

First he got a gallon jar and we went around to the side of the house where the water spigot thrust itself out of the ground like the finger of a saint, surrounded by a mud puddle.

He opened the Kool-Aid and dumped it into the jar. Putting the jar under the spigot, he turned the water on. The water spit, splashed and guzzled out of the spigot.

He was careful to see that the jar did not overflow and the precious Kool-Aid spill out onto the ground. When the jar was full he turned the water off with a sudden but delicate motion like a famous brain surgeon removing a disordered portion of the imagination. Then he screwed the lid tightly onto the top of the jar and gave it a good shake.

The first part of the ceremony was over.

Like the inspired priest of an exotic cult, he had performed the first part of the ceremony well.

His mother came around the side of the house and said in a voice filled with sand and string, "When are you going to do the dishes? . . . Huh?"

"Soon," he said.

"Well, you better," she said.

When she left, it was as if she had never been there at all. The second part of the ceremony began with him carrying the jar very carefully to an abandoned chicken house in the back. "The dishes can wait," he said to me. Bertrand Russell could not have stated it better.

He opened the chicken house door and we went in. The

9

place was littered with half-rotten comic books. They were like fruit under a tree. In the corner was an old mattress and beside the mattress were four quart jars. He took the gallon jar over to them, and filled them carefully not spilling a drop. He screwed their caps on tightly and was now ready for a day's drinking.

You're supposed to make only two quarts of Kool-Aid from a package, but he always made a gallon, so his Kool-Aid was a mere shadow of its desired potency. And you're supposed to add a cup of sugar to every package of Kool-Aid, but he never put any sugar in his Kool-Aid because there wasn't any sugar to put in it.

He created his own Kool-Aid reality and was able to illuminate himself by it.

ANOTHER METHOD
OF MAKING WALNUT CATSUP

And this is a very small cookbook for Trout Fishing in America
as if Trout Fishing in America were a rich gourmet and
Trout Fishing in America had Maria Callas for a girlfriend
and they ate together on a marble table with beautiful candles.

Compote of Apples

Take a dozen of golden pippins, pare them
nicely and take the core out with a small
penknife; put them into some water, and
let them be well scalded; then take a little
of the water with some sugar, and a few
apples which may be sliced into it, and
let the whole boil till it comes to a syrup;
then pour it over your pippins, and garnish
them with dried cherries and lemon-peel
cut fine. You must take care that your
pippins are not split.

And Maria Callas sang to Trout Fishing in America as
they ate their apples together.

A Standing Crust for Great Pies

Take a peck of flour and six pounds of butter
boiled in a gallon of water: skim it off into
the flour, and as little of the liquor as you
can. Work it up well into a paste, and then
pull it into pieces till it is cold. Then make
it up into what form you please.

11

A Spoonful Pudding

Take a spoonful of flour, a spoonful of
cream or milk, an egg, a little nutmeg,
ginger, and salt. Mix all together, and
boil it in a little wooden dish half an hour.
If you think proper you may add a few
currants.

And Trout Fishing in America said, "The moon's coming
out." And Maria Callas said, "Yes, it is."

Another Method of Making Walnut Catsup

Take green walnuts before the shell is
formed, and grind them in a crab-mill,
or pound them in a marble mortar.
Squeeze out the juice through a coarse
cloth, and put to every gallon of juice
a pound of anchovies, and the same
quantity of bay-salt, four ounces of
Jamaica pepper, two of long and two of
black pepper; of mace, cloves, and
ginger, each an ounce, and a stick of
horseradish. Boil all together till
reduced to half the quantity, and then
put it into a pot. When it is cold, bottle
it close, and in three months it will be
fit for use.

And Trout Fishing in America and Maria Callas poured
walnut catsup on their hamburgers.

PROLOGUE TO GRIDER CREEK

Mooresville, Indiana, is the town that John Dillinger came from, and the town has a John Dillinger Museum. You can go in and look around.

Some towns are known as the peach capital of America or the cherry capital or the oyster capital, and there's always a festival and the photograph of a pretty girl in a bathing suit.

Mooresville, Indiana, is the John Dillinger capital of America.

Recently a man moved there with his wife, and he discovered hundreds of rats in his basement. They were huge, slow-moving child-eyed rats.

When his wife had to visit some of her relatives for a few days, the man went out and bought a .38 revolver and a lot of ammunition. Then he went down to the basement where the rats were, and he started shooting them. It didn't bother the rats at all. They acted as if it were a movie and started eating their dead companions for popcorn.

The man walked over to a rat that was busy eating a friend and placed the pistol against the rat's head. The rat did not move and continued eating away. When the hammer clicked back, the rat paused between bites and looked out of the corner of its eye. First at the pistol and then at the man. It was a kind of friendly look as if to say, "When my mother was young she sang like Deanna Durbin."

The man pulled the trigger.

He had no sense of humor.

There's always a single feature, a double feature and an eternal feature playing at the Great Theater in Mooresville, Indiana: the John Dillinger capital of America.

GRIDER CREEK

I had heard there was some good fishing in there and it was running clear while all the other large creeks were running muddy from the snow melting off the Marble Mountains.

I also heard there were some Eastern brook trout in there, high up in the mountains, living in the wakes of beaver dams.

The guy who drove the school bus drew a map of Grider Creek, showing where the good fishing was. We were standing in front of Steelhead Lodge when he drew the map. It was a very hot day. I'd imagine it was a hundred degrees.

You had to have a car to get to Grider Creek where the good fishing was, and I didn't have a car. The map was nice, though. Drawn with a heavy dull pencil on a piece of paper bag. With a little square ☐ for a sawmill.

THE BALLET FOR
TROUT FISHING IN AMERICA

How the Cobra Lily traps insects is a ballet for Trout Fishing in America, a ballet to be performed at the University of California at Los Angeles.

The plant is beside me here on the back porch.

It died a few days after I bought it at Woolworth's. That was months ago, during the presidential election of nineteen hundred and sixty.

I buried the plant in an empty Metrecal can.

The side of the can says, "Metrecal Dietary for Weight Control," and below that reads, "Ingredients: Non-fat milk solids, soya flour, whole milk solids, sucrose, starch, corn oil, coconut oil, yeast, imitation vanilla," but the can's only a graveyard now for a Cobra Lily that has turned dry and brown and has black freckles.

As a kind of funeral wreath, there is a red, white and blue button sticking in the plant and the words on it say, "I'm for Nixon."

The main energy for the ballet comes from a description of the Cobra Lily. The description could be used as a welcome mat on the front porch of hell or to conduct an orchestra of mortuaries with ice-cold woodwinds or be an atomic mailman in the pines, in the pines where the sun never shines.

"Nature has endowed the Cobra Lily with the means of catching its own food. The forked tongue is covered with honey glands which attract the insects upon which it feeds. Once inside the hood, downward pointing hairs prevent the insect from crawling out. The digestive liquids are found in the base of the plant.

"The supposition that it is necessary to feed the Cobra Lily a piece of hamburger or an insect daily is erroneous."

I hope the dancers do a good job of it, they hold our

imagination in their feet, dancing in Los Angeles for Trout
Fishing in America.

A WALDEN POND FOR WINOS

The autumn carried along with it, like the roller coaster of
a flesh-eating plant, port wine and the people who drank that
dark sweet wine, people long since gone, except for me.

Always wary of the police, we drank in the safest place
we could find, the park across from the church.

There were three poplar trees in the middle of the park
and there was a statue of Benjamin Franklin in front of the
trees. We sat there and drank port.

At home my wife was pregnant.

I would call on the telephone after I finished work and say,
"I won't be home for a little while. I'm going to have a drink
with some friends."

The three of us huddled in the park, talking. They were
both broken-down artists from New Orleans where they had
drawn pictures of tourists in Pirate's Alley.

Now in San Francisco, with the cold autumn wind upon
them, they had decided that the future held only two direc-
tions: They were either going to open up a flea circus or
commit themselves to an insane asylum.

So they talked about it while they drank wine.

They talked about how to make little clothes for fleas by
pasting pieces of colored paper on their backs.

They said the way that you trained fleas was to make them
dependent upon you for their food. This was done by letting
them feed off you at an appointed hour.

They talked about making little flea wheelbarrows and
pool tables and bicycles.

They would charge fifty-cents admission for their flea
circus. The business was certain to have a future to it. Per-
haps they would even get on the Ed Sullivan Show.

They of course did not have their fleas yet, but they could
easily be obtained from a white cat.

17

Then they decided that the fleas that lived on Siamese cats would probably be more intelligent than the fleas that lived on just ordinary alley cats. It only made sense that drinking intelligent blood would make intelligent fleas.

And so it went on until it was exhausted and we went and bought another fifth of port wine and returned to the trees and Benjamin Franklin.

Now it was close to sunset and the earth was beginning to cool off in the correct manner of eternity and office girls were returning like penguins from Montgomery Street. They looked at us hurriedly and mentally registered: winos.

Then the two artists talked about committing themselves to an insane asylum for the winter. They talked about how warm it would be in the insane asylum, with television, clean sheets on soft beds, hamburger gravy over mashed potatoes, a dance once a week with the lady kooks, clean clothes, a locked razor and lovely young student nurses.

Ah, yes, there was a future in the insane asylum. No winter spent there could be a total loss.

TOM MARTIN CREEK

I walked down one morning from Steelhead, following the
Klamath River that was high and murky and had the intelli-
gence of a dinosaur. Tom Martin Creek was a small creek
with cold, clear water and poured out of a canyon and
through a culvert under the highway and then into the Klamath.

I dropped a fly in a small pool just below where the creek
flowed out of the culvert and took a nine-inch trout. It was
a good-looking fish and fought all over the top of the pool.

Even though the creek was very small and poured out of
a steep brushy canyon filled with poison oak, I decided to
follow the creek up a ways because I liked the feel and motion
of the creek.

I liked the name, too.

Tom Martin Creek.

It's good to name creeks after people and then later to fol-
low them for a while seeing what they have to offer, what
they know and have made of themselves.

But that creek turned out to be a real son-of-a-bitch. I
had to fight it all the God-damn way: brush, poison oak and
hardly any good places to fish, and sometimes the canyon
was so narrow the creek poured out like water from a faucet.
Sometimes it was so bad that it just left me standing there,
not knowing which way to jump.

You had to be a plumber to fish that creek.

After that first trout I was alone in there. But I didn't
know it until later.

TROUT FISHING ON THE BEVEL

The two graveyards were next to each other on small hills and between them flowed Graveyard Creek, a slow-moving, funeral-procession-on-a-hot-day creek with a lot of fine trout in it.

And the dead didn't mind me fishing there at all.

One graveyard had tall fir trees growing in it, and the grass was kept Peter Pan green all year round by pumping water up from the creek, and the graveyard had fine marble headstones and statues and tombs.

The other graveyard was for the poor and it had no trees and the grass turned a flat-tire brown in the summer and stayed that way until the rain, like a mechanic, began in the late autumn.

There were no fancy headstones for the poor dead. Their markers were small boards that looked like heels of stale bread:

Devoted Slob Father Of

Beloved Worked-to-Death Mother Of

On some of the graves were fruit jars and tin cans with wilted flowers in them:

Sacred

To the Memory

of

John Talbot

Who at the Age of Eighteen

Had His Ass Shot Off

In a Honky-Tonk

November 1, 1936

This Mayonnaise Jar

With Wilted Flowers In It

Was Left Here Six Months Ago

By His Sister

Who Is In

The Crazy Place Now.

Eventually the seasons would take care of their wooden names like a sleepy short-order cook cracking eggs over a grill next to a railroad station. Whereas the well-to-do would have their names for a long time written on marble hors d'oeuvres like horses trotting up the fancy paths to the sky.

I fished Graveyard Creek in the dusk when the hatch was on and worked some good trout out of there. Only the poverty of the dead bothered me.

Once, while cleaning the trout before I went home in the almost night, I had a vision of going over to the poor graveyard and gathering up grass and fruit jars and tin cans and markers and wilted flowers and bugs and weeds and clods and going home and putting a hook in the vise and tying a fly with all that stuff and then going outside and casting it up into the sky, watching it float over clouds and then into the evening star.

SEA, SEA RIDER

The man who owned the bookstore was not magic. He was not a three-legged crow on the dandelion side of the mountain.

He was, of course, a Jew, a retired merchant seaman who had been torpedoed in the North Atlantic and floated there day after day until death did not want him. He had a young wife, a heart attack, a Volkswagen and a home in Marin County. He liked the works of George Orwell, Richard Aldington and Edmund Wilson.

He learned about life at sixteen, first from Dostoevsky and then from the whores of New Orleans.

The bookstore was a parking lot for used graveyards. Thousands of graveyards were parked in rows like cars. Most of the books were out of print, and no one wanted to read them any more and the people who had read the books had died or forgotten about them, but through the organic process of music the books had become virgins again. They wore their ancient copyrights like new maidenheads.

I went to the bookstore in the afternoons after I got off work, during that terrible year of 1959.

He had a kitchen in the back of the store and he brewed cups of thick Turkish coffee in a copper pan. I drank coffee and read old books and waited for the year to end. He had a small room above the kitchen.

It looked down on the bookstore and had Chinese screens in front of it. The room contained a couch, a glass cabinet with Chinese things in it and a table and three chairs. There was a tiny bathroom fastened like a watch fob to the room.

I was sitting on a stool in the bookstore one afternoon reading a book that was in the shape of a chalice. The book had clear pages like gin, and the first page in the book read:

Billy

the Kid

born

November 23,

1859

in

New York

City

The owner of the bookstore came up to me, and put his arm on my shoulder and said, "Would you like to get laid?" His voice was very kind.

"No," I said.

"You're wrong," he said, and then without saying anything else, he went out in front of the bookstore, and stopped a pair of total strangers, a man and a woman. He talked to them for a few moments. I couldn't hear what he was saying. He pointed at me in the bookstore. The woman nodded her head and then the man nodded his head.

They came into the bookstore.

I was embarrassed. I could not leave the bookstore because they were entering by the only door, so I decided to go upstairs and go to the toilet. I got up abruptly and walked to the back of the bookstore and went upstairs to the bathroom, and they followed after me.

I could hear them on the stairs.

I waited for a long time in the bathroom and they waited an equally long time in the other room. They never spoke. When I came out of the bathroom, the woman was lying naked on the couch, and the man was sitting in a chair with his hat on his lap.

"Don't worry about him," the girl said. "These things make no difference to him. He's rich. He has 3,859 Rolls Royces." The girl was very pretty and her body was like a clear mountain river of skin and muscle flowing over rocks of bone and hidden nerves.

"Come to me," she said. "And come inside me for we are Aquarius and I love you."

I looked at the man sitting in the chair. He was not smiling and he did not look sad.

I took off my shoes and all my clothes. The man did not say a word.

The girl's body moved ever so slightly from side to side.

There was nothing else I could do for my body was like birds sitting on a telephone wire strung out down the world, clouds tossing the wires carefully.

I laid the girl.

It was like the eternal 59th second when it becomes a minute and then looks kind of sheepish.

"Good," the girl said, and kissed me on the face.

The man sat there without speaking or moving or sending out any emotion into the room. I guess he <u>was</u> rich and owned 3,859 Rolls Royces.

Afterwards the girl got dressed and she and the man left. They walked down the stairs and on their way out, I heard him say his first words.

"Would you like to go to Ernie's for dinner?"

"I don't know," the girl said. "It's a little early to think about dinner."

Then I heard the door close and they were gone. I got dressed and went downstairs. The flesh about my body felt soft and relaxed like an experiment in functional background music.

The owner of the bookstore was sitting at his desk behind the counter. "I'll tell you what happened up there," he said, in a beautiful anti-three-legged-crow voice, in an anti-dandelion side of the mountain voice.

"What?" I said.

"You fought in the Spanish Civil War. You were a young Communist from Cleveland, Ohio. She was a painter. A New York Jew who was sightseeing in the Spanish Civil War as if it were the Mardi Gras in New Orleans being acted out by Greek statues.

"She was drawing a picture of a dead anarchist when you met her. She asked you to stand beside the anarchist and act as if you had killed him. You slapped her across the face and said something that would be embarrassing for me to repeat.

24

"You both fell very much in love.

"Once while you were at the front she read Anatomy of Melancholy and did 349 drawings of a lemon.

"Your love for each other was mostly spiritual. Neither one of you performed like millionaires in bed.

"When Barcelona fell, you and she flew to England, and then took a ship back to New York. Your love for each other remained in Spain. It was only a war love. You loved only yourselves, loving each other in Spain during the war. On the Atlantic you were different toward each other and became every day more and more like people lost from each other.

"Every wave on the Atlantic was like a dead seagull dragging its driftwood artillery from horizon to horizon.

"When the ship bumped up against America, you departed without saying anything and never saw each other again. The last I heard of you, you were still living in Philadelphia."

"That's what you think happened up there?" I said.

"Partly," he said. "Yes, that's part of it."

He took out his pipe and filled it with tobacco and lit it.

"Do you want me to tell you what else happened up there?" he said.

"Go ahead."

"You crossed the border into Mexico," he said. "You rode your horse into a small town. The people knew who you were and they were afraid of you. They knew you had killed many men with that gun you wore at your side. The town itself was so small that it didn't have a priest.

"When the rurales saw you, they left the town. Tough as they were, they did not want to have anything to do with you. The rurales left.

"You became the most powerful man in town.

"You were seduced by a thirteen-year-old girl, and you and she lived together in an adobe hut, and practically all you did was make love.

"She was slender and had long dark hair. You made love standing, sitting, lying on the dirt floor with pigs and chickens around you. The walls, the floor and even the roof of the hut were coated with your sperm and her come.

"You slept on the floor at night and used your sperm for a pillow and her come for a blanket.

"The people in the town were so afraid of you that they could do nothing.

25

"After a while she started going around town without any clothes on, and the people of the town said that it was not a good thing, and when you started going around without any clothes, and when both of you began making love on the back of your horse in the middle of the zocalo, the people of the town became so afraid that they abandoned the town. It's been abandoned ever since.

"People won't live there.

"Neither of you lived to be twenty-one. It was not necessary.

"See, I do know what happened upstairs," he said. He smiled at me kindly. His eyes were like the shoelaces of a harpsichord.

I thought about what happened upstairs.

"You know what I say is the truth," he said. "For you saw it with your own eyes and traveled it with your own body. Finish the book you were reading before you were interrupted. I'm glad you got laid."

Once resumed, the pages of the book began to speed up and turn faster and faster until they were spinning like wheels in the sea.

THE LAST YEAR THE TROUT
CAME UP HAYMAN CREEK

Gone now the old fart. Hayman Creek was named for
Charles Hayman, a sort of half-assed pioneer in a country
that not many wanted to live in because it was poor and ugly
and horrible. He built a shack, this was in 1876, on a little
creek that drained a worthless hill. After a while the creek
was called Hayman Creek.

Mr. Hayman did not know how to read or write and con-
sidered himself better for it. Mr. Hayman did odd jobs for
years and years and years and years.

Your mule's broke?

Get Mr. Hayman to fix it.

Your fences are on fire?

Get Mr. Hayman to put them out.

Mr. Hayman lived on a diet of stone-ground wheat and
kale. He bought the wheat by the hundred-pound sack and
ground it himself with a mortar and pestle. He grew the kale
in front of his shack and tended the kale as if it were prize-
winning orchids.

During all the time that was his life, Mr. Hayman never
had a cup of coffee, a smoke, a drink or a woman and thought
he'd be a fool if he did.

In the winter a few trout would go up Hayman Creek, but
by early summer the creek was almost dry and there were
no fish in it.

Mr. Hayman used to catch a trout or two and eat raw
trout with his stone-ground wheat and his kale, and then one
day he was so old that he did not feel like working any more,
and he looked so old that the children thought he must be evil
to live by himself, and they were afraid to go up the creek
near his shack.

It didn't bother Mr. Hayman. The last thing in the world
he had any use for were children. Reading and writing and

children were all the same, Mr. Hayman thought, and ground his wheat and tended his kale and caught a trout or two when they were in the creek.

He looked ninety years old for thirty years and then he got the notion that he would die, and did so. The year he died the trout didn't come up Hayman Creek, and never went up the creek again. With the old man dead, the trout figured it was better to stay where they were.

The mortar and pestle fell off the shelf and broke.

The shack rotted away.

And the weeds grew into the kale.

Twenty years after Mr. Hayman's death, some fish and game people were planting trout in the streams around there.

"Might as well put some here," one of the men said.

"Sure," the other one said.

They dumped a can full of trout in the creek and no sooner had the trout touched the water, than they turned their white bellies up and floated dead down the creek.

TROUT DEATH BY PORT WINE

It was not an outhouse resting upon the imagination.

It was reality.

An eleven-inch rainbow trout was killed. Its life taken forever from the waters of the earth, by giving it a drink of port wine.

It is against the natural order of death for a trout to die by having a drink of port wine.

It is all right for a trout to have its neck broken by a fisherman and then to be tossed into the creel or for a trout to die from a fungus that crawls like sugar-colored ants over its body until the trout is in death's sugarbowl.

It is all right for a trout to be trapped in a pool that dries up in the late summer or to be caught in the talons of a bird or the claws of an animal.

Yes, it is even all right for a trout to be killed by pollution, to die in a river of suffocating human excrement.

There are trout that die of old age and their white beards flow to the sea.

All these things are in the natural order of death, but for a trout to die from a drink of port wine, that is another thing.

No mention of it in "The treatyse of fysshynge wyth an angle," in the Boke of St. Albans, published 1496. No mention of it in Minor Tactics of the Chalk Stream, by H. C. Cutcliffe, published in 1910. No mention of it in Truth Is Stranger than Fishin', by Beatrice Cook, published in 1955. No mention of it in Northern Memoirs, by Richard Franck, published in 1694. No mention of it in I Go A-Fishing, by W. C. Prime, published in 1873. No mention of it in Trout Fishing and Trout Flies, by Jim Quick, published in 1957. No mention of it in Certaine Experiments Concerning Fish and Fruite, by John Taverner, published in 1600. No mention of it in A River Never Sleeps, by Roderick L. Haig Brown, published in 1946. No mention of it in Till Fish Us Do Part, by Beatrice Cook, published in 1949. No mention of it in The Flyfisher & the Trout's Point of View, by Col. E. W. Harding, published in 1931. No mention of it in Chalk Stream Studies, by Charles Kingsley, published in 1859. No mention of it in Trout Madness, by Robert Traver, published in 1960.

No mention of it in Sunshine and the Dry Fly, by J. W. Dunne, published in 1924. No mention of it in Just Fishing, by Ray Bergman, published in 1932. No mention of it in Matching the Hatch, by Ernest G. Schwiebert, Jr., published in 1955. No mention of it in The Art of Trout Fishing on Rapid Streams, by H. C. Cutcliffe, published in 1863. No mention of it in Old Flies in New Dresses, by C. E. Walker, published in 1898. No mention of it in Fisherman's Spring, by Roderick L. Haig-Brown, published in 1951. No mention of it in The Determined Angler and the Brook Trout, by Charles Bradford, published in 1916. No mention of it in Women Can Fish, by Chisie Farrington, published in 1951. No mention of it in Tales of the Angler's El Dorado New Zealand, by Zane Grey, published in 1926. No mention of it in The Flyfisher's Guide, by G. C. Bainbridge, published in 1816.

There's no mention of a trout dying by having a drink of port wine anywhere.

To describe the Supreme Executioner: We woke up in the morning and it was dark outside. He came kind of smiling into the kitchen and we ate breakfast.

Fried potatoes and eggs and coffee.

"Well, you old bastard," he said. "Pass the salt."

The tackle was already in the car, so we just got in and drove away. Beginning at the first light of dawn, we hit the road at the bottom of the mountains, and drove up into the dawn.

The light behind the trees was like going into a gradual and strange department store.

"That was a good-looking girl last night," he said.

"Yeah," I said. "You did all right."

"If the shoe fits . . ." he said.

Owl Snuff Creek was just a small creek, only a few miles long, but there were some nice trout in it. We got out of the car and walked a quarter of a mile down the mountainside to

30

the creek. I put my tackle together. He pulled a pint of port wine out of his jacket pocket and said, "Wouldn't you know."

"No thanks," I said.

He took a good snort and then shook his head, side to side, and said, "Do you know what this creek reminds me of?"

"No," I said, tying a gray and yellow fly onto my leader.

"It reminds me of Evangeline's vagina, a constant dream of my childhood and promoter of my youth."

"That's nice," I said.

"Longfellow was the Henry Miller of my childhood," he said.

"Good," I said.

I cast into a little pool that had a swirl of fir needles going around the edge of it. The fir needles went around and around. It made no sense that they should come from trees. They looked perfectly contented and natural in the pool as if the pool had grown them on watery branches.

I had a good hit on my third cast, but missed it.

"Oh, boy," he said. "I think I'll watch you fish. The stolen painting is in the house next door."

I fished upstream coming ever closer and closer to the narrow staircase of the canyon. Then I went up into it as if I were entering a department store. I caught three trout in the lost and found department. He didn't even put his tackle together. He just followed after me, drinking port wine and poking a stick at the world.

"This is a beautiful creek," he said. "It reminds me of Evangeline's hearing aid."

We ended up at a large pool that was formed by the creek crashing through the children's toy section. At the beginning of the pool the water was like cream, then it mirrored out and reflected the shadow of a large tree. By this time the sun was up. You could see it coming down the mountain.

I cast into the cream and let my fly drift down onto a long branch of the tree, next to a bird.

Go-wham!

I set the hook and the trout started jumping.

"Giraffe races at Kilimanjaro!" he shouted, and every time the trout jumped, he jumped.

"Bee races at Mount Everest!" he shouted.

I didn't have a net with me so I fought the trout over to the edge of the creek and swung it up onto the shore.

The trout had a big red stripe down its side.

It was a good rainbow.

"What a beauty," he said.

He picked it up and it was squirming in his hands.

"Break its neck," I said.

"I have a better idea," he said. "Before I kill it, let me
at least soothe its approach into death. This trout needs a
drink." He took the bottle of port out of his pocket, unscrewed
the cap and poured a good slug into the trout's mouth.

The trout went into a spasm.

Its body shook very rapidly like a telescope during an
earthquake. The mouth was wide open and chattering almost
as if it had human teeth.

He laid the trout on a white rock, head down, and some
of the wine trickled out of its mouth and made a stain on the
rock.

The trout was lying very still now.

"It died happy," he said.

"This is my ode to Alcoholics Anonymous.

"Look here!"

THE AUTOPSY OF
TROUT FISHING IN AMERICA

This is the autopsy of Trout Fishing in America as if Trout
Fishing in America had been Lord Byron and had died in
Missolonghi, Greece, and afterward never saw the shores
of Idaho again, never saw Carrie Creek, Worsewick Hot
Springs, Paradise Creek, Salt Creek and Duck Lake again.

The Autopsy of Trout Fishing in America:

"The body was in excellent state and appeared as one that
had died suddenly of asphyxiation. The bony cranial vault
was opened and the bones of the cranium were found very
hard without any traces of the sutures like the bones of a
person 80 years, so much so that one would have said that
the cranium was formed by one solitary bone. . . . The
meninges were attached to the internal walls of the cranium
so firmly that while sawing the bone around the interior to
detach the bone from the dura the strength of two robust men
was not sufficient. . . . The cerebrum with cerebellum
weighed about six medical pounds. The kidneys were very
large but healthy and the urinary bladder was relatively
small."

On May 2, 1824, the body of Trout Fishing in America
left Missolonghi by ship destined to arrive in England on the
evening of June 29, 1824.

Trout Fishing in America's body was preserved in a cask
holding one hundred-eighty gallons of spirits: O, a long way
from Idaho, a long way from Stanley Basin, Little Redfish
Lake, the Big Lost River and from Lake Josephus and the
Big Wood River.

THE MESSAGE

Last night a blue thing, the smoke itself, from our campfire
drifted down the valley, entering into the sound of the bell-
mare until the blue thing and the bell could not be separated,
no matter how hard you tried. There was no crowbar big
enough to do the job.

Yesterday afternoon we drove down the road from Wells
Summit, then we ran into the sheep. They also were being
moved on the road.

A shepherd walked in front of the car, a leafy branch in
his hand, sweeping the sheep aside. He looked like a young,
skinny Adolf Hitler, but friendly.

I guess there were a thousand sheep on the road. It was
hot and dusty and noisy and took what seemed like a long
time.

At the end of the sheep was a covered wagon being pulled
by two horses. There was a third horse, the bellmare, tied
on the back of the wagon. The white canvas rippled in the
wind and the wagon had no driver. The seat was empty.

Finally the Adolf Hitler, but friendly, shepherd got the
last of them out of the way. He smiled and we waved and said
thank you.

We were looking for a good place to camp. We drove down
the road, following the Little Smoky about five miles and
didn't see a place that we liked, so we decided to turn around
and go back to a place we had seen just a ways up Carrie
Creek.

"I hope those God-damn sheep aren't on the road," I said.

We drove back to where we had seen them on the road
and, of course, they were gone, but as we drove on up the
road, we just kept following sheep shit. It was ahead of us
for the next mile.

I kept looking down on the meadow by the Little Smoky, hoping to see the sheep down there, but there wasn't a sheep in sight, only the shit in front of us on the road.

As if it were a game invented by the sphincter muscle, we knew what the score was. Shaking our heads side to side, waiting.

Then we went around a bend and the sheep burst like a roman candle all over the road and again a thousand sheep and the shepherd in front of us, wondering what the fuck. The same thing was in our minds.

There was some beer in the back seat. It wasn't exactly cold, but it wasn't warm either. I tell you I was really embarrassed. I took a bottle of beer and got out of the car.

I walked up to the shepherd who looked like Adolf Hitler, but friendly.

"I'm sorry," I said.

"It's the sheep," he said. (O sweet and distant blossoms of Munich and Berlin!) "Sometimes they are a trouble but it all works out."

"Would you like a bottle of beer?" I said. "I'm sorry to put you through this again."

"Thank you," he said, shrugging his shoulders. He took the beer over and put it on the empty seat of the wagon. That's how it looked. After a long time, we were free of the sheep. They were like a net dragged finally away from the car.

We drove up to the place on Carrie Creek and pitched the tent and took our goods out of the car and piled them in the tent.

Then we drove up the creek a ways, above the place where there were beaver dams and the trout stared back at us like fallen leaves.

We filled the back of the car with wood for the fire and I caught a mess of those leaves for dinner. They were small and dark and cold. The autumn was good to us.

When we got back to our camp, I saw the shepherd's wagon down the road a ways and on the meadow I heard the bellmare and the very distant sound of the sheep.

It was the final circle with the Adolf Hitler, but friendly, shepherd as the diameter. He was camping down there for the night. So in the dusk, the blue smoke from our campfire went down and got in there with the bellmare.

35

The sheep lulled themselves into senseless sleep, one following another like the banners of a lost army. I have here a very important message that just arrived a few moments ago. It says "Stalingrad."

TROUT FISHING IN AMERICA
TERRORISTS

Long live our friend the revolver!
Long live our friend the machine-gun!

—Israeli terrorist chant

One April morning in the sixth grade, we became, first by
accident and then by premeditation, trout fishing in America
terrorists.

It came about this way: we were a strange bunch of kids.

We were always being called in before the principal for
daring and mischievous deeds. The principal was a young
man and a genius in the way he handled us.

One April morning we were standing around in the play
yard, acting as if it were a huge open-air poolhall with the
first-graders coming and going like pool balls. We were all
bored with the prospect of another day's school, studying
Cuba.

One of us had a piece of white chalk and as a first-grader
went walking by, the one of us absentmindedly wrote "Trout
fishing in America" on the back of the first-grader.

The first-grader strained around, trying to read what was
written on his back, but he couldn't see what it was, so he
shrugged his shoulders and went off to play on the swings.

We watched the first-grader walk away with "Trout fish-
ing in America" written on his back. It looked good and
seemed quite natural and pleasing to the eye that a first-
grader should have "Trout fishing in America" written in
chalk on his back.

The next time I saw a first-grader, I borrowed my friend's
piece of chalk and said, "First-grader, you're wanted over
here."

37

The first-grader came over to me and I said, "Turn around."

The first-grader turned around and I wrote "Trout fishing in America" on his back. It looked even better on the second first-grader. We couldn't help but admire it. "Trout fishing in America." It certainly did add something to the first-graders. It completed them and gave them a kind of class.

"It really looks good, doesn't it?"

"Yeah."

"Let's get some more chalk."

"Sure."

"There are a lot of first-graders over there by the monkey-bars."

"Yeah."

We all got hold of chalk and later in the day, by the end of lunch period, almost all of the first-graders had "Trout fishing in America" written on their backs, girls included.

Complaints began arriving at the principal's office from the first-grade teachers. One of the complaints was in the form of a little girl.

"Miss Robins sent me," she said to the principal. "She told me to have you look at this."

"Look at what?" the principal said, staring at the empty child.

"At my back," she said.

The little girl turned around and the principal read aloud, "Trout fishing in America."

"Who did this?" the principal said.

"That gang of sixth-graders," she said. "The bad ones. They've done it to all us first-graders. We all look like this. 'Trout fishing in America.' What does it mean? I just got this sweater new from my grandma."

"Huh. 'Trout fishing in America,'" the principal said."Tell Miss Robins I'll be down to see her in a little while," and excused the girl and a short time later we terrorists were summoned up from the lower world.

We reluctantly stamped into the principal's office, fidgeting and pawing our feet and looking out the windows and yawning and one of us suddenly got an insane blink going and putting our hands into our pockets and looking away and then back again and looking up at the light fixture on the ceiling, how much it looked like a boiled potato, and down again and at the

picture of the principal's mother on the wall. She had been a
star in the silent pictures and was tied to a railroad track.

"Does 'Trout fishing in America' seem at all familiar to
you boys?" the principal said. "I wonder if perhaps you've
seen it written down anywhere today in your travels? 'Trout
fishing in America.' Think hard about it for a minute."

We all thought hard about it.

There was a silence in the room, a silence that we all
knew intimately, having been at the principal's office quite a
few times in the past.

"Let me see if I can help you," the principal said. "Per-
haps you saw 'Trout fishing in America' written in chalk on
the backs of the first-graders. I wonder how it got there."

We couldn't help but smile nervously.

"I just came back from Miss Robin's first-grade class,"
the principal said. "I asked all those who had 'Trout fishing
in America' written on their backs to hold up their hands, and
all the children in the class held up their hands, except one
and he had spent his whole lunch period hiding in the lavatory.
What do you boys make of it . . . ? This 'Trout fishing in
America' business?"

We didn't say anything.

The one of us still had his mad blink going. I am certain
that it was his guilty blink that always gave us away. We
should have gotten rid of him at the beginning of the sixth
grade.

"You're all guilty, aren't you?" he said. "Is there one of
you who isn't guilty? If there is, speak up. Now."

We were all silent except for blink, blink, blink, blink, blink.
Suddenly I could _hear_ his God-damn eye blinking. It was very much
like the sound of an insect laying the 1,000,000th egg of our
disaster.

"The whole bunch of you did it. Why? . . . Why 'Trout
fishing in America' on the backs of the first-graders?"

And then the principal went into his famous $E=MC^2$ sixth-
grade gimmick, the thing he always used in dealing with us.

"Now wouldn't it look funny," he said. "If I asked all your
teachers to come in here, and then I told the teachers all to
turn around, and then I took a piece of chalk and wrote 'Trout
fishing in America' on their backs?"

We all giggled nervously and blushed faintly.

"Would you like to see your teachers walking around all
day with 'Trout fishing in America' written on their backs,

trying to teach you about Cuba? That would look silly, wouldn't it? You wouldn't like to see that, would you? That wouldn't do at all, would it?"

"No," we said like a Greek chorus, some of us saying it with our voices and some of us by nodding our heads, and then there was the blink, blink, blink.

"That's what I thought," he said. "The first-graders look up to you and admire you like the teachers look up to me and admire me. It just won't do to write 'Trout fishing in America' on their backs. Are we agreed, gentlemen?"

We were agreed.

I tell you it worked every God-damn time.

Of course it had to work.

"All right," he said. "I'll consider trout fishing in America to have come to an end. Agreed?"

"Agreed."

"Agreed?"

"Agreed."

"Blink, blink."

But it wasn't completely over, for it took a while to get trout fishing in America off the clothes of the first-graders. A fair percentage of trout fishing in America was gone the next day. The mothers did this by simply putting clean clothes on their children, but there were a lot of kids whose mothers just tried to wipe it off and then sent them back to school the next day with the same clothes on, but you could still see "Trout fishing in America" faintly outlined on their backs. But after a few more days trout fishing in America disappeared altogether as it was destined to from its very beginning, and a kind of autumn fell over the first grade.

TROUT FISHING IN AMERICA

WITH THE FBI

Dear Trout Fishing in America,

last week walking along lower market on the way to work saw the pictures of the FBI's TEN MOST WANTED MEN in the window of a store. the dodger under one of the pictures was folded under at both sides and you couldn't read all of it. the picture showed a nice, clean-cut-looking guy with freckles and curly (red?) hair

WANTED FOR:
RICHARD LAWRENCE MARQUETTE
Aliases: Richard Lawrence Marquette, Richard
Lourence Marquette
Description:
26, born Dec. 12, 1934, Portland, Oregon
170 to 180 pounds
muscular
light brown, cut short
blue
Complexion: ruddy
Race: white
Nationality: American
Occupations: auto body w
recapper, s
survey rod
arks: 6" hernia scar; tattoo "Mom" in wreath on ight forearm
ull upper denture, may also have lower denture.
Reportedly frequents
s, and is an avid trout fisherman.

41

(this is how the dodger looked cut off on both sides and you couldn't make out any more, even what he was wanted for.)

Your old buddy,

Pard

Dear Pard,

Your letter explains why I saw two FBI agents watching a trout stream last week. They watched a path that came down through the trees and then circled a large black stump and led to a deep pool. Trout were rising in the pool. The FBI agents watched the path, the trees, the black stump, the pool and the trout as if they were all holes punched in a card that had just come out of a computer. The afternoon sun kept changing everything as it moved across the sky, and the FBI agents kept changing with the sun. It appears to be part of their training.

Your friend,

Trout Fishing in America

WORSEWICK

Worsewick Hot Springs was nothing fancy. Somebody put some boards across the creek. That was it.

The boards dammed up the creek enough to form a huge bathtub there, and the creek flowed over the top of the boards, invited like a postcard to the ocean a thousand miles away.

As I said Worsewick was nothing fancy, not like the places where the swells go. There were no buildings around. We saw an old shoe lying by the tub.

The hot springs came down off a hill and where they flowed there was a bright orange scum through the sagebrush. The hot springs flowed into the creek right there at the tub and that's where it was nice.

We parked our car on the dirt road and went down and took off our clothes, then we took off the baby's clothes, and the deerflies had at us until we got into the water, and then they stopped.

There was a green slime growing around the edges of the tub and there were dozens of dead fish floating in our bath. Their bodies had been turned white by death, like frost on iron doors. Their eyes were large and stiff.

The fish had made the mistake of going down the creek too far and ending up in hot water, singing, "When you lose your money, learn to lose."

We played and relaxed in the water. The green slime and the dead fish played and relaxed with us and flowed out over us and entwined themselves about us.

Splashing around in that hot water with my woman, I began to get ideas, as they say. After a while I placed my body in such a position in the water that the baby could not see my hard-on.

I did this by going deeper and deeper in the water, like a

43

dinosaur, and letting the green slime and dead fish cover me over.

My woman took the baby out of the water and gave her a bottle and put her back in the car. The baby was tired. It was really time for her to take a nap.

My woman took a blanket out of the car and covered up the windows that faced the hot springs. She put the blanket on top of the car and then lay rocks on the blanket to hold it in place. I remember her standing there by the car.

Then she came back to the water, and the deerflies were at her, and then it was my turn. After a while she said, "I don't have my diaphragm with me and besides it wouldn't work in the water, anyway. I think it's a good idea if you don't come inside me. What do you think?"

I thought this over and said all right. I didn't want any more kids for a long time. The green slime and dead fish were all about our bodies.

I remember a dead fish floated under her neck. I waited for it to come up on the other side, and it came up on the other side.

Worsewick was nothing fancy.

Then I came, and just cleared her in a split second like an airplane in the movies, pulling out of a nosedive and sailing over the roof of a school.

My sperm came out into the water, unaccustomed to the light, and instantly it became a misty, stringy kind of thing and swirled out like a falling star, and I saw a dead fish come forward and float into my sperm, bending it in the middle. His eyes were stiff like iron.

THE SHIPPING OF TROUT
FISHING IN AMERICA SHORTY
TO NELSON ALGREN

Trout Fishing in America Shorty appeared suddenly last autumn in San Francisco, staggering around in a magnificent chrome-plated steel wheelchair.

He was a legless, screaming middle-aged wino.

He descended upon North Beach like a chapter from the Old Testament. He was the reason birds migrate in the autumn. They have to. He was the cold turning of the earth; the bad wind that blows off sugar.

He would stop children on the street and say to them, "I ain't got no legs. The trout chopped my legs off in Fort Lauderdale. You kids got legs. The trout didn't chop your legs off. Wheel me into that store over there."

The kids, frightened and embarrassed, would wheel Trout Fishing in America Shorty into the store. It would always be a store that sold sweet wine, and he would buy a bottle of wine and then he'd have the kids wheel him back out onto the street, and he would open the wine and start drinking there on the street just like he was Winston Churchill.

After a while the children would run and hide when they saw Trout Fishing in America Shorty coming.

"I pushed him last week,"

"I pushed him yesterday,"

"Quick, let's hide behind these garbage cans."

And they would hide behind the garbage cans while Trout Fishing in America Shorty staggered by in his wheelchair. The kids would hold their breath until he was gone.

Trout Fishing in America Shorty used to go down to L'Italia, the Italian newspaper in North Beach at Stockton and Green Streets. Old Italians gather in front of the newspaper in the afternoon and just stand there, leaning up against the building, talking and dying in the sun.

45

Trout Fishing in America Shorty used to wheel into the middle of them as if they were a bunch of pigeons, bottle of wine in hand, and begin shouting obscenities in fake Italian.

Tra-la-la-la-la-la-Spa-ghet-tiii!

I remember Trout Fishing in America Shorty passed out in Washington Square, right in front of the Benjamin Franklin statue. He had fallen face first out of his wheelchair and just lay there without moving.

Snoring loudly.

Above him were the metal works of Benjamin Franklin like a clock, hat in hand.

Trout Fishing in America Shorty lay there below, his face spread out like a fan in the grass.

A friend and I got to talking about Trout Fishing in America Shorty one afternoon. We decided the best thing to do with him was to pack him in a big shipping crate with a couple of cases of sweet wine and send him to Nelson Algren.

Nelson Algren is always writing about Railroad Shorty, a hero of the Neon Wilderness (the reason for "The Face on the Barroom Floor") and the destroyer of Dove Linkhorn in A Walk on the Wild Side.

We thought that Nelson Algren would make the perfect custodian for Trout Fishing in America Shorty. Maybe a museum might be started. Trout Fishing in America Shorty could be the first piece in an important collection.

We would nail him up in a packing crate with a big label on it.

Contents:
Trout Fishing in America Shorty

Occupation:
Wino

Address:
C/O Nelson Algren
Chicago

And there would be stickers all over the crate, saying: "GLASS/HANDLE WITH CARE/SPECIAL HANDLING/GLASS /DON'T SPILL/THIS SIDE UP/HANDLE THIS WINO LIKE HE WAS AN ANGEL"

And Trout Fishing in America Shorty, grumbling, puking and cursing in his crate would travel across America, from San Francisco to Chicago.

46

And Trout Fishing in America Shorty, wondering what it was all about, would travel on, shouting, "Where in the hell am I? I can't see to open this bottle! Who turned out the lights? Fuck this motel! I have to take a piss! Where's my key?"

It was a good idea.

A few days after we made our plans for Trout Fishing in America Shorty, a heavy rain was pouring down upon San Francisco. The rain turned the streets inward, like drowned lungs, upon themselves and I was hurrying to work, meeting swollen gutters at the intersections.

I saw Trout Fishing in America Shorty passed out in the front window of a Filipino laundromat. He was sitting in his wheelchair with closed eyes staring out the window.

There was a tranquil expression on his face. He almost looked human. He had probably fallen asleep while he was having his brains washed in one of the machines.

Weeks passed and we never got around to shipping Trout Fishing in America Shorty away to Nelson Algren. We kept putting it off. One thing and another. Then we lost our golden opportunity because Trout Fishing in America Shorty disappeared a little while after that.

They probably swept him up one morning and put him in jail to punish him, the evil fart, or they put him in a nuthouse to dry him out a little.

Maybe Trout Fishing in America Shorty just pedaled down to San Jose in his wheelchair, rattling along the freeway at a quarter of a mile an hour.

I don't know what happened to him. But if he comes back to San Francisco someday and dies, I have an idea.

Trout Fishing in America Shorty should be buried right beside the Benjamin Franklin statue in Washington Square. We should anchor his wheelchair to a huge gray stone and write upon the stone:

Trout Fishing in America Shorty
20¢ Wash
10¢ Dry
Forever

THE MAYOR

OF THE TWENTIETH CENTURY

London. On December 1, 1887; July 7, August 8, September 30, one day in the month of October and on the 9th of November, 1888; on the 1st of June, the 17th of July and the 10th of September 1889 . . .

The disguise was perfect.

Nobody ever saw him, except, of course, the victims. They saw him.

Who would have expected?

He wore a costume of trout fishing in America. He wore mountains on his elbows and bluejays on the collar of his shirt. Deep water flowed through the lilies that were entwined about his shoelaces. A bullfrog kept croaking in his watch pocket and the air was filled with the sweet smell of ripe blackberry bushes.

He wore trout fishing in America as a costume to hide his own appearance from the world while he performed his deeds of murder in the night.

Who would have expected?

Nobody!

Scotland Yard?

(Pouf!)

They were always a hundred miles away, wearing halibut-stalker hats, looking under the dust.

Nobody ever found out.

O, now he's the Mayor of the Twentieth Century! A razor, a knife and a ukelele are his favorite instruments.

Of course, it would have to be a ukelele. Nobody else would have thought of it, pulled like a plow through the intestines.

ON PARADISE

"Speaking of evacuations, your missive, while complete in
other regards, skirted the subject, though you did deal brief-
ly with rural micturition procedure. I consider this a gross
oversight on your part, as I'm certain you're well aware of
my unending fascination with camp-out crapping. Please
rush details in your next effort. Slit-trench, pith helmet,
slingshot, biffy and if so number of holes and proximity of
keester to vermin and deposits of prior users."

—From a Letter by a Friend

Sheep. Everything smelled of sheep on Paradise Creek,
but there were no sheep in sight. I fished down from the
ranger station where there was a huge monument to the Civi-
lian Conservation Corps.

It was a twelve-foot high marble statue of a young man
walking out on a cold morning to a crapper that had the clas-
sic half-moon cut above the door.

The 1930s will never come again, but his shoes were
wet with dew. They'll stay that way in marble.

I went off into the marsh. There the creek was soft and
spread out in the grass like a beer belly. The fishing was
difficult. Summer ducks were jumping up into flight. They
were big mallards with their Rainier Ale-like offspring.

I believe I saw a woodcock. He had a long bill like putting
a fire hydrant into a pencil sharpener, then pasting it onto
a bird and letting the bird fly away in front of me with this
thing on its face for no other purpose than to amaze me.

I worked my way slowly out of the marsh until the creek
again became a muscular thing, the strongest Paradise
Creek in the world. I was then close enough to see the sheep.
There were hundreds of them.

Everything smelled of sheep. The dandelions were sudden-
ly more sheep than flower, each petal reflecting wool and
the sound of a bell ringing off the yellow. But the thing that
smelled the most like sheep, was the very sun itself. When
the sun went behind a cloud, the smell of the sheep decreased,
like standing on some old guy's hearing aid, and when the
sun came back again, the smell of the sheep was loud, like
a clap of thunder inside a cup of coffee.

That afternoon the sheep crossed the creek in front of
my hook. They were so close that their shadows fell across
my bait. I practically caught trout up their assholes.

THE CABINET OF
DOCTOR CALIGARI

Once water bugs were my field. I remember that childhood spring when I studied the winter-long mud puddles of the Pacific Northwest. I had a fellowship.

My books were a pair of Sears Roebuck boots, ones with green rubber pages. Most of my classrooms were close to the shore. That's where the important things were happening and that's where the good things were happening.

Sometimes as experiments I laid boards out into the mud puddles, so I could look into the deeper water but it was not nearly as good as the water in close to the shore.

The water bugs were so small I practically had to lay my vision like a drowned orange on the mud puddle. There is a romance about fruit floating outside on the water, about apples and pears in rivers and lakes. For the first minute or so, I saw nothing, and then slowly the water bugs came into being.

I saw a black one with big teeth chasing a white one with a bag of newspapers slung over its shoulder, two white ones playing cards near the window, a fourth white one staring back with a harmonica in its mouth.

I was a scholar until the mud puddles went dry and then I picked cherries for two-and-a-half cents a pound in an old orchard that was beside a long, hot dusty road.

The cherry boss was a middle-aged woman who was a real Okie. Wearing a pair of goofy overalls, her name was Rebel Smith, and she'd been a friend of "Pretty Boy" Floyd's down in Oklahoma. "I remember one afternoon 'Pretty Boy' came driving up in his car. I ran out onto the front porch."

Rebel Smith was always smoking cigarettes and showing people how to pick cherries and assigning them to trees and writing down everything in a little book she carried in her shirt pocket. She smoked just half a cigarette and then threw

51

the other half on the ground.

For the first few days of the picking, I was always seeing her half-smoked cigarettes lying all over the orchard, near the john and around the trees and down the rows.

Then she hired half-a-dozen bums to pick cherries because the picking was going too slowly. Rebel picked the bums up on skidrow every morning and drove them out to the orchard in a rusty old truck. There were always half-a-dozen bums, but sometimes they had different faces.

After they came to pick cherries I never saw any more of her half-smoked cigarettes lying around. They were gone before they hit the ground. Looking back on it, you might say that Rebel Smith was anti-mud puddle, but then you might not say that at all.

THE SALT CREEK COYOTES

High and lonesome and steady, it's the smell of sheep down
in the valley that has done it to them. Here all afternoon in
the rain I've been listening to the sound of the coyotes up on
Salt Creek.

The smell of the sheep grazing in the valley has done it
to them. Their voices water and come down the canyon, past
the summer homes. Their voices are a creek, running down
the mountain, over the bones of sheep, living and dead.

O, THERE ARE COYOTES UP ON SALT CREEK so the
sign on the trail says, and it also says, WATCH OUT FOR
CYANIDE CAPSULES PUT ALONG THE CREEK TO KILL
COYOTES. DON'T PICK THEM UP AND EAT THEM. NOT
UNLESS YOU'RE A COYOTE. THEY'LL KILL YOU. LEAVE
THEM ALONE.

Then the sign says this all over again in Spanish. ¡AH!
HAY COYOTES EN SALT CREEK, TAMBIEN. CUIDADO
CON LAS CAPSULAS DE CIANURO: MATAN. NO LAS
COMA; A MENOS QUE SEA VD. UN COYOTE. MATAN.
NO LAS TOQUE.

It does not say it in Russian.

I asked an old guy in a bar about those cyanide capsules
up on Salt Creek and he told me that they were a kind of pis-
tol. They put a pleasing coyote scent on the trigger (prob-
ably the smell of a coyote snatch) and then a coyote comes
along and gives it a good sniff, a fast feel and BLAM! That's
all, brother.

I went fishing up on Salt Creek and caught a nice little
Dolly Varden trout, spotted and slender as a snake you'd ex-
pect to find in a jewelry store, but after a while I could think
only of the gas chamber at San Quentin.

O Caryl Chessman and Alexander Robillard Vistas! as if
they were names for tracts of three-bedroom houses with

53

wall-to-wall carpets and plumbing that defies the imagination.

Then it came to me up there on Salt Creek, capital punishment being what it is, an act of state business with no song down the railroad track after the train has gone and no vibration on the rails, that they should take the head of a coyote killed by one of those God-damn cyanide things up on Salt Creek and hollow it out and dry it in the sun and then make it into a crown with the teeth running in a circle around the top of it and a nice green light coming off the teeth.

Then the witnesses and newspapermen and gas chamber flunkies would have to watch a king wearing a coyote crown die there in front of them, the gas rising in the chamber like a rain mist drifting down the mountain from Salt Creek. It has been raining here now for two days, and through the trees, the heart stops beating.

THE HUNCHBACK TROUT

The creek was made narrow by little green trees that grew too close together. The creek was like 12, 845 telephone booths in a row with high Victorian ceilings and all the doors taken off and all the backs of the booths knocked out.

Sometimes when I went fishing in there, I felt just like a telephone repairman, even though I did not look like one. I was only a kid covered with fishing tackle, but in some strange way by going in there and catching a few trout, I kept the telephones in service. I was an asset to society.

It was pleasant work, but at times it made me uneasy. It could grow dark in there instantly when there were some clouds in the sky and they worked their way onto the sun. Then you almost needed candles to fish by, and foxfire in your reflexes.

Once I was in there when it started raining. It was dark and hot and steamy. I was of course on overtime. I had that going in my favor. I caught seven trout in fifteen minutes.

The trout in those telephone booths were good fellows. There were a lot of young cutthroat trout six to nine inches long, perfect pan size for local calls. Sometimes there were a few fellows, eleven inches or so—for the long distance calls.

I've always liked cutthroat trout. They put up a good fight, running against the bottom and then broad jumping. Under their throats they fly the orange banner of Jack the Ripper.

Also in the creek were a few stubborn rainbow trout, seldom heard from, but there all the same, like certified public accountants. I'd catch one every once in a while. They were fat and chunky, almost as wide as they were long. I've heard those trout called "squire" trout.

It used to take me about an hour to hitchhike to that creek. There was a river nearby. The river wasn't much. The creek

55

was where I punched in. Leaving my card above the clock, I'd punch out again when it was time to go home.

I remember the afternoon I caught the hunchback trout.

A farmer gave me a ride in a truck. He picked me up at a traffic signal beside a bean field and he never said a word to me.

His stopping and picking me up and driving me down the road was as automatic a thing to him as closing the barn door, nothing need be said about it, but still I was in motion traveling thirty-five miles an hour down the road, watching houses and groves of trees go by, watching chickens and mailboxes enter and pass through my vision.

Then I did not see any houses for a while. "This is where I get out," I said.

The farmer nodded his head. The truck stopped.

"Thanks a lot," I said.

The farmer did not ruin his audition for the Metropolitan Opera by making a sound. He just nodded his head again. The truck started up. He was the original silent old farmer.

A little while later I was punching in at the creek. I put my card above the clock and went into that long tunnel of telephone booths.

I waded about seventy-three telephone booths in. I caught two trout in a little hole that was like a wagon wheel. It was one of my favorite holes, and always good for a trout or two.

I always like to think of that hole as a kind of pencil sharpener. I put my reflexes in and they came back out with a good point on them. Over a period of a couple of years, I must have caught fifty trout in that hole, though it was only as big as a wagon wheel.

I was fishing with salmon eggs and using a size 14 single egg hook on a pound and a quarter test tippet. The two trout lay in my creel covered entirely by green ferns, ferns made gentle and fragile by the damp walls of telephone booths.

The next good place was forty-five telephone booths in. The place was at the end of a run of gravel, brown and slippery with algae. The run of gravel dropped off and disappeared at a little shelf where there were some white rocks.

One of the rocks was kind of strange. It was a flat white rock. Off by itself from the other rocks, it reminded me of a white cat I had seen in my childhood.

The cat had fallen or been thrown off a high wooden sidewalk that went along the side of a hill in Tacoma, Washington. The cat was lying in a parking lot below.

The fall had not appreciably helped the thickness of the cat, and then a few people had parked their cars on the cat. Of course, that was a long time ago and the cars looked different from the way they look now.

You hardly see those cars any more. They are the old cars. They have to get off the highway because they can't keep up.

That flat white rock off by itself from the other rocks reminded me of that dead cat come to lie there in the creek, among 12,845 telephone booths.

I threw out a salmon egg and let it drift down over that rock and WHAM! a good hit! and I had the fish on and it ran hard downstream, cutting at an angle and staying deep and really coming on hard, solid and uncompromising, and then the fish jumped and for a second I thought it was a frog. I'd never seen a fish like that before.

God-damn! What the hell!

The fish ran deep again and I could feel its life energy screaming back up the line to my hand. The line felt like sound. It was like an ambulance siren coming straight at me, red light flashing, and then going away again and then taking to the air and becoming an air-raid siren.

The fish jumped a few more times and it still looked like a frog, but it didn't have any legs. Then the fish grew tired and sloppy, and I swung and splashed it up the surface of the creek and into my net.

The fish was a twelve-inch rainbow trout with a huge hump on its back. A hunchback trout. The first I'd ever seen. The hump was probably due to an injury that occurred when the trout was young. Maybe a horse stepped on it or a tree fell over in a storm or its mother spawned where they were building a bridge.

There was a fine thing about that trout. I only wish I could have made a death mask of him. Not of his body though, but of his energy. I don't know if anyone would have understood his body. I put it in my creel.

Later in the afternoon when the telephone booths began to grow dark at the edges, I punched out of the creek and went home. I had that hunchback trout for dinner. Wrapped in cornmeal and fried in butter, its hump tasted sweet as the kisses of Esmeralda.

THE TEDDY ROOSEVELT

CHINGADER'

<u>The Challis National Forest was created July 1, 1908, by
Executive Order of President Theodore Roosevelt . . .
Twenty Million years ago, scientists tell us, three-toed
horses, camels, and possibly rhinoceroses were plentiful
in this section of the country.</u>

This is part of my history in the Challis National Forest.
We came over through Lowman after spending a little time
with my woman's Mormon relatives at McCall, where we
learned about Spirit Prison and couldn't find Duck Lake.

I carried the baby up the mountain. The sign said $1^1/2$
miles. There was a green sports car parked on the road.
We walked up the trail until we met a man with a green
sports car hat on and a girl in a light summer dress.

She had her dress rolled above her knees and when she
saw us coming, she rolled her dress down. The man had a
bottle of wine in his back pocket. The wine was in a long
green bottle. It looked funny sticking out of his back pocket.

"How far is it to Spirit Prison?" I asked.

"You're about half way," he said.

The girl smiled. She had blonde hair and they went on
down. Bounce, bounce, bounce, like a pair of birthday balls,
down through the trees and boulders.

I put the baby down in a patch of snow lying in the hollow
behind a big stump. She played in the snow and then started
eating it. I remembered something from a book by Justice
of the Supreme Court, William O. Douglas. DON'T EAT
SNOW. IT'S BAD FOR YOU AND WILL GIVE YOU A STOM-
ACH ACHE.

"Stop eating that snow!" I said to the baby.

I put her on my shoulders and continued up the path toward
Spirit Prison. That's where everybody who isn't a Mormon

goes when they die. All Catholics, Buddhists, Moslems, Jews, Baptists, Methodists and International Jewel Thieves. Everybody who isn't a Mormon goes to the Spirit Slammer.

The sign said $1^1/2$ miles. The path was easy to follow, then it just stopped. We lost it near a creek. I looked all around. I looked on both sides of the creek, but the path had just vanished.

Could be the fact that we were still alive had something to do with it. Hard to tell.

We turned around and started back down the mountain. The baby cried when she saw the snow again, holding out her hands for the snow. We didn't have time to stop. It was getting late.

We got in our car and drove back to McCall. That evening we talked about Communism. The Mormon girl read aloud to us from a book called The Naked Communist written by an ex-police chief of Salt Lake City.

My woman asked the girl if she believed the book were written under the influence of Divine Power, if she considered the book to be a religious text of some sort.

The girl said, "No."

I bought a pair of tennis shoes and three pairs of socks at a store in McCall. The socks had a written guarantee. I tried to save the guarantee, but I put it in my pocket and lost it. The guarantee said that if anything happened to the socks within three months time, I would get new socks. It seemed like a good idea.

I was supposed to launder the old socks and send them in with the guarantee. Right off the bat, new socks would be on their way, traveling across America with my name on the package. Then all I would have to do, would be to open the package, take those new socks out and put them on. They would look good on my feet.

I wish I hadn't lost that guarantee. That was a shame. I've had to face the fact that new socks are not going to be a family heirloom. Losing the guarantee took care of that. All future generations are on their own.

We left McCall the next day, the day after I lost the sock guarantee, following the muddy water of the North Fork of the Payette down and the clear water of the South Fork up.

We stopped at Lowman and had a strawberry milkshake and then drove back into the mountains along Clear Creek and over the summit to Bear Creek.

There were signs nailed to the trees all along Bear Creek, the signs said, "IF YOU FISH IN THIS CREEK, WE'LL HIT YOU IN THE HEAD." I didn't want to be hit in the head, so I kept my fishing tackle right there in the car.

We saw a flock of sheep. There's a sound that the baby makes when she sees furry animals. She also makes that sound when she sees her mother and me naked. She made that sound and we drove out of the sheep like an airplane flies out of the clouds.

We entered Challis National Forest about five miles away from that sound. Driving now along Valley Creek, we saw the Sawtooth Mountains for the first time. It was clouding over and we thought it was going to rain.

"Looks like it's raining in Stanley," I said, though I had never been in Stanley before. It is easy to say things about Stanley when you have never been there. We saw the road to Bull Trout Lake. The road looked good. When we reached Stanley, the streets were white and dry like a collision at a high rate of speed between a cemetery and a truck loaded with sacks of flour.

We stopped at a store in Stanley. I bought a candy bar and asked how the trout fishing was in Cuba. The woman at the store said, "You're better off dead, you Commie bastard." I got a receipt for the candy bar to be used for income tax purposes.

The old ten-cent deduction.

I didn't learn anything about fishing in that store. The people were awfully nervous, especially a young man who was folding overalls. He had about a hundred pairs left to fold and he was really nervous.

We went over to a restaurant and I had a hamburger and my woman had a cheeseburger and the baby ran in circles like a bat at the World's Fair.

There was a girl there in her early teens or maybe she was only ten years old. She wore lipstick and had a loud voice and seemed to be aware of boys. She got a lot of fun out of sweeping the front porch of the restaurant.

She came in and played around with the baby. She was very good with the baby. Her voice dropped down and got soft with the baby. She told us that her father'd had a heart attack and was still in bed. "He can't get up and around," she said.

We had some more coffee and I thought about the Mormons.
That very morning we had said good-bye to them, after having
drunk coffee in their house.

The smell of coffee had been like a spider web in the
house. It had not been an easy smell. It had not lent itself to
religious contemplation, thoughts of temple work to be done
in Salt Lake, dead relatives to be discovered among ancient
papers in Illinois and Germany. Then more temple work to
be done in Salt Lake.

The Mormon woman told us that when she had been mar-
ried in the temple at Salt Lake, a mosquito had bitten her on
the wrist just before the ceremony and her wrist had swollen
up and become huge and just awful. It could've been seen
through the lace by a blindman. She had been so embarrassed.

She told us that those Salt Lake mosquitoes always made
her swell up when they bit her. Last year, she had told us,
she'd been in Salt Lake, doing some temple work for a dead
relative when a mosquito had bitten her and her whole body
had swollen up. "I felt so embarrassed," she had told us.
"Walking around like a balloon."

We finished our coffee and left. Not a drop of rain had fal-
len in Stanley. It was about an hour before sundown.

We drove up to Big Redfish Lake, about four miles from
Stanley and looked it over. Big Redfish Lake is the Forest
Lawn of camping in Idaho, laid out for maximum comfort.
There were a lot of people camped there, and some of them
looked as if they had been camped there for a long time.

We decided that we were too young to camp at Big Redfish
Lake, and besides they charged fifty cents a day, three dol-
lars a week like a skidrow hotel, and there were just too
many people there. There were too many trailers and camp-
ers parked in the halls. We couldn't get to the elevator be-
cause there was a family from New York parked there in a
ten-room trailer.

Three children came by drinking rub-a-dub and pulling
an old granny by her legs. Her legs were straight out and
stiff and her butt was banging on the carpet. Those kids were
pretty drunk and the old granny wasn't too sober either, shout-
ing something like, "Let the Civil War come again, I'm ready
to fuck!"

We went down to Little Redfish Lake. The campgrounds
there were just about abandoned. There were so many people

up at Big Redfish Lake and practically nobody camping at Little Redfish Lake, and it was free, too.

We wondered what was wrong with the camp. If perhaps a camping plague, a sure destroyer that leaves all your camping equipment, your car and your sex organs in tatters like old sails, had swept the camp just a few days before, and those few people who were staying at the camp now, were staying there because they didn't have any sense.

We joined them enthusiastically. The camp had a beautiful view of the mountains. We found a place that really looked good, right on the lake.

Unit 4 had a stove. It was a square metal box mounted on a cement block. There was a stove pipe on top of the box, but there were no bullet holes in the pipe. I was amazed. Almost all the camp stoves we had seen in Idaho had been full of bullet holes. I guess it's only reasonable that people, when they get the chance, would want to shoot some old stove sitting in the woods.

Unit 4 had a big wooden table with benches attached to it like a pair of those old Benjamin Franklin glasses, the ones with those funny square lenses. I sat down on the left lens, facing the Sawtooth Mountains. Like astigmatism, I made myself at home.

FOOTNOTE CHAPTER TO "THE SHIPPING OF TROUT FISHING IN AMERICA SHORTY TO NELSON ALGREN"

Well, well, Trout Fishing in America Shorty's back in town, but I don't think it's going to be the same as it was before. Those good old days are over because Trout Fishing in America Shorty is famous. The movies have discovered him.

Last week "The New Wave" took him out of his wheelchair and laid him out in a cobblestone alley. Then they shot some footage of him. He ranted and raved and they put it down on film.

Later on, probably, a different voice will be dubbed in. It will be a noble and eloquent voice denouncing man's inhumanity to man in no uncertain terms.

"Trout Fishing in America Shorty, Mon Amour."

His soliloquy beginning with, "I was once a famous skiptracer known throughout America as 'Grasshopper Nijinsky.' Nothing was too good for me. Beautiful blondes followed me wherever I went." Etc. . . . They'll milk it for all it's worth and make cream and butter from a pair of empty pants legs and a low budget.

But I may be all wrong. What was being shot may have been just a scene from a new science-fiction movie "Trout Fishing in America Shorty from Outer Space." One of those cheap thrillers with the theme: Scientists, mad-or-otherwise, should never play God, that ends with the castle on fire and a lot of people walking home through the dark woods.

THE PUDDING MASTER OF
STANLEY BASIN

Tree, snow and rock beginnings, the mountain in back of the lake promised us eternity, but the lake itself was filled with thousands of silly minnows, swimming close to the shore and busy putting in hours of Mack Sennett time.

The minnows were an Idaho tourist attraction. They should have been made into a National Monument. Swimming close to shore, like children, they believed in their own immortality.

A third-year student in engineering at the University of Montana attempted to catch some of the minnows but he went about it all wrong. So did the children who came on the Fourth of July weekend.

The children waded out into the lake and tried to catch the minnows with their hands. They also used milk cartons and plastic bags. They presented the lake with hours of human effort. Their total catch was one minnow. It jumped out of a can full of water on their table and died under the table, gasping for watery breath while their mother fried eggs on the Coleman stove.

The mother apologized. She was supposed to be watching the fish —THIS IS MY EARTHLY FAILURE— holding the dead fish by the tail, the fish taking all the bows like a young Jewish comedian talking about Adlai Stevenson.

The third-year student in engineering at the University of Montana took a tin can and punched an elaborate design of holes in the can, the design running around and around in circles, like a dog with a fire hydrant in its mouth. Then he attached some string to the can and put a huge salmon egg and a piece of Swiss cheese in the can. After two hours of intimate and universal failure, he went back to Missoula, Montana.

The woman who travels with me discovered the best way to catch the minnows. She used a large pan that had in its bottom the dregs of a distant vanilla pudding. She put the pan in the shallow water along the shore and instantly, hundreds of minnows gathered around. Then, mesmerized by the vanilla pudding, they swam like a children's crusade into the pan. She caught twenty fish with one dip. She put the pan full of fish on the shore and the baby played with the fish for an hour.

We watched the baby to make sure she was just leaning on them a little. We didn't want her to kill any of them because she was too young.

Instead of making her furry sound, she adapted rapidly to the difference between animals and fish, and was soon making a silver sound.

She caught one of the fish with her hand and looked at it for a while. We took the fish out of her hand and put it back into the pan. After a while she was putting the fish back by herself.

Then she grew tired of this. She tipped the pan over and a dozen fish flopped out onto the shore. The children's game and the banker's game, she picked up those silver things, one at a time, and put them back in the pan. There was still a little water in it. The fish liked this. You could tell.

When she got tired of the fish, we put them back in the lake, and they were all quite alive, but nervous. I doubt if they will ever want vanilla pudding again.

ROOM 208, HOTEL

TROUT FISHING IN AMERICA

Half a block from Broadway and Columbus is Hotel Trout
Fishing in America, a cheap hotel. It is very old and run by
some Chinese. They are young and ambitious Chinese and
the lobby is filled with the smell of Lysol.

The Lysol sits like another guest on the stuffed furniture,
reading a copy of the Chronicle, the Sports Section. It is the
only furniture I have ever seen in my life that looks like baby
food.

And the Lysol sits asleep next to an old Italian pensioner
who listens to the heavy ticking of the clock and dreams of
eternity's golden pasta, sweet basil and Jesus Christ.

The Chinese are always doing something to the hotel. One
week they paint a lower banister and the next week they put
some new wallpaper on part of the third floor.

No matter how many times you pass that part of the third
floor, you cannot remember the color of the wallpaper or
what the design is. All you know is that part of the wallpaper
is new. It is different from the old wallpaper. But you can-
not remember what that looks like either.

One day the Chinese take a bed out of a room and lean it
up against the wall. It stays there for a month. You get used
to seeing it and then you go by one day and it is gone. You
wonder where it went.

I remember the first time I went inside Hotel Trout Fish-
ing in America. It was with a friend to meet some people.

"I'll tell you what's happening," he said. "She's an ex-
hustler who works for the telephone company. He went to
medical school for a while during the Great Depression and
then he went into show business. After that, he was an errand
boy for an abortion mill in Los Angeles. He took a fall and
did some time in San Quentin.

"I think you'll like them. They're good people.

"He met her a couple of years ago in North Beach. She
was hustling for a spade pimp. It's kind of weird. Most
women have the temperament to be a whore, but she's one
of these rare women who just don't have it—the whore tem-
perament. She's Negro, too.

"She was a teenage girl living on a farm in Oklahoma. The
pimp drove by one afternoon and saw her playing in the front
yard. He stopped his car and got out and talked to her father
for a while.

"I guess he gave her father some money. He came up
with something good because her father told her to go and
get her things. So she went with the pimp. Simple as that.

"He took her to San Francisco and turned her out and she
hated it. He kept her in line by terrorizing her all the time.
He was a real sweetheart.

"She had some brains, so he got her a job with the tele-
phone company during the day, and he had her hustling at
night.

"When Art took her away from him, he got pretty mad. A
good thing and all that. He used to break into Art's hotel
room in the middle of the night and put a switchblade to Art's
throat and rant and rave. Art kept putting bigger and bigger
locks on the door, but the pimp just kept breaking in—a huge
fellow.

"So Art went out and got a .32 pistol, and the next time
the pimp broke in, Art pulled the gun out from underneath
the covers and jammed it into the pimp's mouth and said,
'You'll be out of luck the next time you come through that
door, Jack.' This broke the pimp up. He never went back.
The pimp certainly lost a good thing.

"He ran up a couple thousand dollars worth of bills in her
name, charge accounts and the like. They're still paying
them off.

"The pistol's right there beside the bed, just in case the
pimp has an attack of amnesia and wants to have his shoes
shined in a funeral parlor.

"When we go up there, he'll drink the wine. She won't.
She'll have a little bottle of brandy. She won't offer us any
of it. She drinks about four of them a day. Never buys a fifth.
She always keeps going out and getting another half-pint.

"That's the way she handles it. She doesn't talk very much,

67

and she doesn't make any bad scenes. A good-looking woman."

My friend knocked on the door and we could hear somebody get up off the bed and come to the door.

"Who's there?" said a man on the other side.

"Me," my friend said, in a voice deep and recognizable as any name.

"I'll open the door." A simple declarative sentence. He undid about a hundred locks, bolts and chains and anchors and steel spikes and canes filled with acid, and then the door opened like the classroom of a great university and everything was in its proper place: the gun beside the bed and a small bottle of brandy beside an attractive Negro woman.

There were many flowers and plants growing in the room, some of them were on the dresser, surrounded by old photographs. All of the photographs were of white people, including Art when he was young and handsome and looked just like the 1930s.

There were pictures of animals cut out of magazines and tacked to the wall, with crayola frames drawn around them and crayola picture wires drawn holding them to the wall. They were pictures of kittens and puppies. They looked just fine.

There was a bowl of goldfish next to the bed, next to the gun. How religious and intimate the goldfish and the gun looked together.

They had a cat named 208. They covered the bathroom floor with newspaper and the cat crapped on the newspaper. My friend said that 208 thought he was the only cat left in the world, not having seen another cat since he was a tiny kitten. They never let him out of the room. He was a red cat and very aggressive. When you played with that cat, he really bit you. Stroke 208's fur and he'd try to disembowel your hand as if it were a belly stuffed full of extrasoft intestines.

We sat there and drank and talked about books. Art had owned a lot of books in Los Angeles, but they were all gone now. He told us that he used to spend his spare time in secondhand bookstores buying old and unusual books when he was in show business, traveling from city to city across America. Some of them were very rare autographed books, he told us, but he had bought them for very little and was forced to sell them for very little.

"They'd be worth a lot of money now," he said.

The Negro woman sat there very quietly studying her brandy. A couple of times she said yes, in a sort of nice way. She used the word yes to its best advantage, when surrounded by no meaning and left alone from other words.

They did their own cooking in the room and had a single hot plate sitting on the floor, next to half a dozen plants, including a peach tree growing in a coffee can. Their closet was stuffed with food. Along with shirts, suits and dresses, were canned goods, eggs and cooking oil.

My friend told me that she was a very fine cook. That she could really cook up a good meal, fancy dishes, too, on that single hot plate, next to the peach tree.

They had a good world going for them. He had such a soft voice and manner that he worked as a private nurse for rich mental patients. He made good money when he worked, but sometimes he was sick himself. He was kind of run down. She was still working for the telephone company, but she wasn't doing that night work any more.

They were still paying off the bills that pimp had run up. I mean, years had passed and they were still paying them off: a Cadillac and a hi fi set and expensive clothes and all those things that Negro pimps do love to have.

I went back there half a dozen times after that first meeting. An interesting thing happened. I pretended that the cat, 208, was named after their room number, though I knew that their number was in the three hundreds. The room was on the third floor. It was that simple.

I always went to their room following the geography of Hotel Trout Fishing in America, rather than its numerical layout. I never knew what the exact number of their room was. I knew secretly it was in the three hundreds and that was all.

Anyway, it was easier for me to establish order in my mind by pretending that the cat was named after their room number. It seemed like a good idea and the logical reason for a cat to have the name 208. It, of course, was not true. It was a fib. The cat's name was 208 and the room number was in the three hundreds.

Where did the name 208 come from? What did it mean? I thought about it for a while, hiding it from the rest of my mind. But I didn't ruin my birthday by secretly thinking about it too hard.

A year later I found out the true significance of 208's name, purely by accident. My telephone rang one Saturday morning when the sun was shining on the hills. It was a close friend of mine and he said, "I'm in the slammer. Come and get me out. They're burning black candles around the drunk tank."

I went down to the Hall of Justice to bail my friend out, and discovered that 208 is the room number of the bail office. It was very simple. I paid ten dollars for my friend's life and found the original meaning of 208, how it runs like melting snow all the way down the mountainside to a small cat living and playing in Hotel Trout Fishing in America, believing itself to be the last cat in the world, not having seen another cat in such a long time, totally unafraid, newspaper spread out all over the bathroom floor, and something good cooking on the hot plate.

THE SURGEON

I watched my day begin on Little Redfish Lake as clearly as
the first light of dawn or the first ray of the sunrise, though
the dawn and the sunrise had long since passed and it was
now late in the morning.

The surgeon took a knife from the sheath at his belt and
cut the throat of the chub with a very gentle motion, showing
poetically how sharp the knife was, and then he heaved the
fish back out into the lake.

The chub made an awkward dead splash and obeyed all the
traffic laws of this world SCHOOL ZONE SPEED 25 MILES
and sank to the cold bottom of the lake. It lay there white
belly up like a school bus covered with snow. A trout swam
over and took a look, just putting in time, and swam away.

The surgeon and I were talking about the AMA. I don't
know how in the hell we got on the thing, but we were on it.
Then he wiped the knife off and put it back in the sheath. I
actually don't know how we got on the AMA.

The surgeon said that he had spent twenty-five years be-
coming a doctor. His studies had been interrupted by the
Depression and two wars. He told me that he would give up
the practice of medicine if it became socialized in America.

"I've never turned away a patient in my life, and I've
never known another doctor who has. Last year I wrote off
six thousand dollars worth of bad debts," he said.

I was going to say that a sick person should never under
any conditions be a bad debt, but I decided to forget it. Noth-
ing was going to be proved or changed on the shores of Little
Redfish Lake, and as that chub had discovered, it was not a
good place to have cosmetic surgery done.

"I worked three years ago for a union in Southern Utah
that had a health plan," the surgeon said. "I would not care

71

to practice medicine under such conditions. The patients think they own you and your time. They think you're their own personal garbage can.

"I'd be home eating dinner and the telephone would ring, 'Help! Doctor! I'm dying! It's my stomach! I've got horrible pains!' I would get up from my dinner and rush over there.

"The guy would meet me at the door with a can of beer in his hand. 'Hi, doc, come on in. I'll get you a beer. I'm watching TV. The pain's all gone. Great, huh? I feel like a million. Sit down. I'll get you a beer, doc. The Ed Sullivan Show's on.'

"No thank you," the surgeon said. "I wouldn't care to practice medicine under such conditions. No thank you. No thanks.

"I like to hunt and I like to fish," he said. "That's why I moved to Twin Falls. I'd heard so much about Idaho hunting and fishing. I've been very disappointed. I've given up my practice, sold my home in Twin, and now I'm looking for a new place to settle down.

"I've written to Montana, Wyoming, Colorado, New Mexico, Arizona, California, Nevada, Oregon and Washington for their hunting and fishing regulations, and I'm studying them all," he said.

"I've got enough money to travel around for six months, looking for a place to settle down where the hunting and fishing is good. I'll get twelve hundred dollars back in income tax returns by not working any more this year. That's two hundred a month for not working. I don't understand this country," he said.

The surgeon's wife and children were in a trailer nearby. The trailer had come in the night before, pulled by a brand-new Rambler station wagon. He had two children, a boy two-and-a-half years old and the other, an infant born prematurely, but now almost up to normal weight.

The surgeon told me that they'd come over from camping on Big Lost River where he had caught a fourteen-inch brook trout. He was young looking, though he did not have much hair on his head.

I talked to the surgeon for a little while longer and said good-bye. We were leaving in the afternoon for Lake Josephus, located at the edge of the Idaho Wilderness, and he was leaving for America, often only a place in the mind.

A NOTE ON THE CAMPING

CRAZE THAT IS CURRENTLY

SWEEPING AMERICA

As much as anything else, the Coleman lantern is the sym-
bol of the camping craze that is currently sweeping America,
with its unholy white light burning in the forests of America.

Last summer, a Mr. Norris was drinking at a bar in San
Francisco. It was Sunday night and he'd had six or seven.
Turning to the guy on the next stool, he said, "What are you
up to?"

"Just having a few," the guy said.

"That's what I'm doing," Mr. Norris said. "I like it."

"I know what you mean," the guy said. "I had to lay off
for a couple years. I'm just starting up again."

"What was wrong?" Mr. Norris said.

"I had a hole in my liver," the guy said.

"In your liver?"

"Yeah, the doctor said it was big enough to wave a flag
in. It's better now. I can have a couple once in a while. I'm
not supposed to, but it won't kill me."

"Well, I'm thirty-two years old," Mr. Norris said. "I've
had three wives and I can't remember the names of my child-
ren."

The guy on the next stool, like a bird on the next island,
took a sip from his Scotch and soda. The guy liked the sound
of the alcohol in his drink. He put the glass back on the bar.

"That's no problem," he said to Mr. Norris. "The best
thing I know for remembering the names of children from
previous marriages, is to go out camping, try a little trout
fishing. Trout fishing is one of the best things in the world
for remembering children's names."

"Is that right?" Mr. Norris said.

"Yeah," the guy said.

"That sounds like an idea," Mr. Norris said. "I've got to
do something. Sometimes I think one of them is named Carl,

73

but that's impossible. My third-ex hated the name Carl."

"You try some camping and that trout fishing," the guy on the next stool said. "And you'll remember the names of your unborn children."

"Carl! Carl! Your mother wants you!" Mr. Norris yelled as a kind of joke, then he realized that it wasn't very funny. He was getting there.

He'd have a couple more and then his head would always fall forward and hit the bar like a gunshot. He'd always miss his glass, so he wouldn't cut his face. His head would always jump up and look startled around the bar, people staring at it. He'd get up then, and take it home.

The next morning Mr. Norris went down to a sporting goods store and charged his equipment. He charged a 9 x 9 foot dry finish tent with an aluminum center pole. Then he charged an Arctic sleeping bag filled with eiderdown and an air mattress and an air pillow to go with the sleeping bag. He also charged an air alarm clock to go along with the idea of night and waking in the morning.

He charged a two-burner Coleman stove and a Coleman lantern and a folding aluminum table and a big set of interlocking aluminum cookware and a portable ice box.

The last things he charged were his fishing tackle and a bottle of insect repellent.

He left the next day for the mountains.

Hours later, when he arrived in the mountains, the first sixteen campgrounds he stopped at were filled with people. He was a little surprised. He had no idea the mountains would be so crowded.

At the seventeenth campground, a man had just died of a heart attack and the ambulance attendants were taking down his tent. They lowered the center pole and then pulled up the corner stakes. They folded the tent neatly and put it in the back of the ambulance, right beside the man's body.

They drove off down the road, leaving behind them in the air, a cloud of brilliant white dust. The dust looked like the light from a Coleman lantern.

Mr. Norris pitched his tent right there and set up all his equipment and soon had it all going at once. After he finished eating a dehydrated beef Stroganoff dinner, he turned off all his equipment with the master air switch and went to sleep, for it was now dark.

74

It was about midnight when they brought the body and placed it beside the tent, less than a foot away from where Mr. Norris was sleeping in his Arctic sleeping bag.

He was awakened when they brought the body. They weren't exactly the quietest body bringers in the world. Mr. Norris could see the bulge of the body against the side of the tent. The only thing that separated him from the dead body was a thin layer of 6 oz. water resistant and mildew resistant DRY FINISH green AMERIFLEX poplin.

Mr. Norris un-zipped his sleeping bag and went outside with a gigantic hound-like flashlight. He saw the body bringers walking down the path toward the creek.

"Hey, you guys!" Mr. Norris shouted. "Come back here. You forgot something."

"What do you mean?" one of them said. They both looked very sheepish, caught in the teeth of the flashlight.

"You know what I mean," Mr. Norris said. "Right now!"

The body bringers shrugged their shoulders, looked at each other and then reluctantly went back, dragging their feet like children all the way. They picked up the body. It was heavy and one of them had trouble getting hold of the feet.

That one said, kind of hopelessly to Mr. Norris, "You won't change your mind?"

"Goodnight and good-bye," Mr. Norris said.

They went off down the path toward the creek, carrying the body between them. Mr. Norris turned his flashlight off and he could hear them, stumbling over the rocks along the bank of the creek. He could hear them swearing at each other. He heard one of them say, "Hold your end up." Then he couldn't hear anything.

About ten minutes later he saw all sorts of lights go on at another campsite down along the creek. He heard a distant voice shouting, "The answer is no! You already woke up the kids. They have to have their rest. We're going on a four-mile hike tomorrow up to Fish Konk Lake. Try someplace else."

A RETURN TO THE COVER OF
THIS BOOK

Dear Trout Fishing in America:

I met your friend Fritz in Washington Square. He told me
to tell you that his case went to a jury and that he was acquit-
ted by the jury.

He said that it was important for me to say that his case
went to a jury and that he was acquitted by the jury, so I've
said it again.

He looked in good shape. He was sitting in the sun. There's
an old San Francisco saying that goes: "It's better to rest in
Washington Square than in the California Adult Authority."

How are things in New York?

Yours,

"An Ardent Admirer"

Dear Ardent Admirer:

It's good to hear that Fritz isn't in jail. He was very wor-
ried about it. The last time I was in San Francisco, he told
me he thought the odds were 10-1 in favor of him going away.
I told him to get a good lawyer. It appears that he followed
my advice and also was very lucky. That's always a good
combination.

You asked about New York and New York is very hot.

I'm visiting some friends, a young burglar and his wife.
He's unemployed and his wife is working as a cocktail wait-
ress. He's been looking for work but I fear the worst.

It was so hot last night that I slept with a wet sheet wrapped
around myself, trying to keep cool. I felt like a mental patient.

I woke up in the middle of the night and the room was filled
with steam rising off the sheet, and there was jungle stuff,

76

abandoned equipment and tropical flowers, on the floor and on the furniture.

I took the sheet into the bathroom and plopped it into the tub and turned the cold water on it. Their dog came in and started barking at me.

The dog barked so loud that the bathroom was soon filled with dead people. One of them wanted to use my wet sheet for a shroud. I said no, and we got into a big argument over it and woke up the Puerto Ricans in the next apartment, and they began pounding on the walls.

The dead people all left in a huff. "We know when we're not wanted," one of them said.

"You're damn tootin'," I said.

I've had enough.

I'm going to get out of New York. Tomorrow I'm leaving for Alaska. I'm going to find an ice-cold creek near the Arctic where that strange beautiful moss grows and spend a week with the grayling. My address will be, Trout Fishing in America, c/o General Delivery, Fairbanks, Alaska.

Your friend,

Trout Fishing in America

THE LAKE JOSEPHUS DAYS

We left Little Redfish for Lake Josephus, traveling along the
good names—from Stanley to Capehorn to Seafoam to the
Rapid River, up Float Creek, past the Greyhound Mine and
then to Lake Josephus, and a few days after that up the trail
to Hell-diver Lake with the baby on my shoulders and a good
limit of trout waiting in Hell-diver.

Knowing the trout would wait there like airplane tickets
for us to come, we stopped at Mushroom Springs and had a
drink of cold shadowy water and some photographs taken of
the baby and me sitting together on a log.

I hope someday we'll have enough money to get those pic-
tures developed. Sometimes I get curious about them, won-
dering if they will turn out all right. They are in suspension
now like seeds in a package. I'll be older when they are de-
veloped and easier to please. Look there's the baby! Look
there's Mushroom Springs! Look there's me!

I caught the limit of trout within an hour of reaching Hell-
diver, and my woman, in all the excitement of good fishing,
let the baby fall asleep directly in the sun and when the baby
woke up, she puked and I carried her back down the trail.

My woman trailed silently behind, carrying the rods and
the fish. The baby puked a couple more times, thimblefuls
of gentle lavender vomit, but still it got on my clothes, and
her face was hot and flushed.

We stopped at Mushroom Springs. I gave her a small
drink of water, not too much, and rinsed the vomit taste out
of her mouth. Then I wiped the puke off my clothes and for
some strange reason suddenly it was a perfect time, there
at Mushroom Springs, to wonder whatever happened to the
Zoot suit.

Along with World War II and the Andrews Sisters, the
Zoot suit had been very popular in the early 40s. I guess

they were all just passing fads.

A sick baby on the trail down from Hell-diver, July 1961, is probably a more important question. It cannot be left to go on forever, a sick baby to take her place in the galaxy, among the comets, bound to pass close to the earth every 173 years.

She stopped puking after Mushroom Springs, and I carried her back down along the path in and out of the shadows and across other nameless springs, and by the time we got down to Lake Josephus, she was all right.

She was soon running around with a big cutthroat trout in her hands, carrying it like a harp on her way to a concert— ten minutes late with no bus in sight and no taxi either.

TROUT FISHING

ON THE STREET OF ETERNITY

Calle de Eternidad: We walked up from Gelatao, birthplace of Benito Juarez. Instead of taking the road we followed a path up along the creek. Some boys from the school in Gelatao told us that up along the creek was the shortcut.

The creek was clear but a little milky, and as I remember the path was steep in places. We met people coming down the path because it was really the shortcut. They were all Indians carrying something.

Finally the path went away from the creek and we climbed a hill and arrived at the cemetery. It was a very old cemetery and kind of run down with weeds and death growing there like partners in a dance.

There was a cobblestone street leading up from the cemetery to the town of Ixtlan, pronounced East-LON, on top of another hill. There were no houses along the street until you reached the town.

In the hair of the world, the street was very steep as you went up into Ixtlan. There was a street sign that pointed back down toward the cemetery, following every cobblestone with loving care all the way.

We were still out of breath from the climb. The sign said Calle de Eternidad. Pointing.

I was not always a world traveler, visiting exotic places in Southern Mexico. Once I was just a kid working for an old woman in the Pacific Northwest. She was in her nineties and I worked for her on Saturdays and after school and during the summer.

Sometimes she would make me lunch, little egg sandwiches with the crusts cut off as if by a surgeon, and she'd give me slices of banana dunked in mayonnaise.

The old woman lived by herself in a house that was like a

80

twin sister to her. The house was four stories high and had
at least thirty rooms and the old lady was five feet high and
weighed about eighty-two pounds.

She had a big radio from the 1920s in the living room and
it was the only thing in the house that looked remotely as if
it had come from this century, and then there was still a
doubt in my mind.

A lot of cars, airplanes and vacuum cleaners and refrig-
erators and things that come from the 1920s look as if they
had come from the 1890s. It's the beauty of our speed that
has done it to them, causing them to age prematurely into the
clothes and thoughts of people from another century.

The old woman had an old dog, but he hardly counted any
more. He was so old that he looked like a stuffed dog. Once
I took him for a walk down to the store. It was just like tak-
ing a stuffed dog for a walk. I tied him up to a stuffed fire
hydrant and he pissed on it, but it was only stuffed piss.

I went into the store and bought some stuffing for the old
lady. Maybe a pound of coffee or a quart of mayonnaise.

I did things for her like chop the Canadian thistles. Dur-
ing the 1920s (or was it the 1890s) she was motoring in Cali-
fornia, and her husband stopped the car at a filling station
and told the attendant to fill it up.

"How about some wild flower seeds?" the attendant said.

"No," her husband said. "Gasoline."

"I know that, sir," the attendant said. "But we're giving
away wild flower seeds with the gasoline today."

"All right," her husband said. "Give us some wild flower
seeds, then. But be sure and fill the car up with gasoline.
Gasoline's what I really want."

"They'll brighten up your garden, sir."

"The gasoline?"

"No, sir, the flowers."

They returned to the Northwest, planted the seeds and
they were Canadian thistles. Every year I chopped them down
and they always grew back. I poured chemicals on them and
they always grew back.

Curses were music to their roots. A blow on the back of
the neck was like a harpsichord to them. Those Canadian
thistles were there for keeps. Thank you, California, for
your beautiful wild flowers. I chopped them down every year.

I did other things for her like mow the lawn with a grim

old lawnmower. When I first went to work for her, she told
me to be careful with that lawnmower. Some itinerant had
stopped at her place a few weeks before, asked for some
work so he could rent a hotel room and get something to eat,
and she'd said, "You can mow the lawn."

"Thanks, ma'am," he'd said and went out and promptly
cut three fingers off his right hand with that medieval mach-
ine.

I was always very careful with that lawnmower, knowing
that somewhere on that place, the ghosts of three fingers
were living it up in the grand spook manner. They needed no
company from my fingers. My fingers looked just great, right
there on my hands.

I cleaned out her rock garden and deported snakes when-
ever I found them on her place. She told me to kill them, but
I couldn't see any percentage in wasting a gartersnake. But
I had to get rid of the things because she always promised me
she'd have a heart attack if she ever stepped on one of them.

So I'd catch them and deport them to a yard across the
street, where nine old ladies probably had heart attacks and
died from finding those snakes in their toothbrushes. Fortu-
nately, I was never around when their bodies were taken away.

I'd clean the blackberry bushes out of the lilac bushes.
Once in a while she'd give me some lilacs to take home, and
they were always fine-looking lilacs, and I always felt good,
walking down the street, holding the lilacs high and proud
like glasses of that famous children's drink: the good flower
wine.

I'd chop wood for her stove. She cooked on a woodstove
and heated the place during the winter with a huge wood fur-
nace that she manned like the captain of a submarine in a
dark basement ocean during the winter.

In the summer I'd throw endless cords of wood into her
basement until I was silly in the head and everything looked
like wood, even clouds in the sky and cars parked on the
street and cats.

There were dozens of little tiny things that I did for her.
Find a lost screwdriver, lost in 1911. Pick her a pan full of
pie cherries in the spring, and pick the rest of the cherries
on the tree for myself. Prune those goofy, at best half-assed
trees in the backyard. The ones that grew beside an old pile
of lumber. Weed.

82

One early autumn day she loaned me to the woman next door and I fixed a small leak in the roof of her woodshed. The woman gave me a dollar tip, and I said thank you, and the next time it rained, all the newspapers she had been saving for seventeen years to start fires with got soaking wet. From then on out, I received a sour look every time I passed her house. I was lucky I wasn't lynched.

I didn't work for the old lady in the winter. I'd finish the year by the last of October, raking up leaves or something or transporting the last muttering gartersnake to winter quarters in the old ladies' toothbrush Valhalla across the street.

Then she'd call me on the telephone in the spring. I would always be surprised to hear her little voice, surprised that she was still alive. I'd get on my horse and go out to her place and the whole thing would begin again and I'd make a few bucks and stroke the sun-warmed fur of her stuffed dog.

One spring day she had me ascend to the attic and clean up some boxes of stuff and throw out some stuff and put some stuff back into its imaginary proper place.

I was up there all alone for three hours. It was my first time up there and my last, thank God. The attic was stuffed to the gills with stuff.

Everything that's old in this world was up there. I spent most of my time just looking around.

An old trunk caught my eye. I unstrapped the straps, unclicked the various clickers and opened the God-damn thing. It was stuffed with old fishing tackle. There were old rods and reels and lines and boots and creels and there was a metal box full of flies and lures and hooks.

Some of the hooks still had worms on them. The worms were years and decades old and petrified to the hooks. The worms were now as much a part of the hooks as the metal itself.

There was some old Trout Fishing in America armor in the trunk and beside a weather-beaten fishing helmet, I saw an old diary. I opened the diary to the first page and it said:

The Trout Fishing Diary of Alonso Hagen

It seemed to me that was the name of the old lady's brother who had died of a strange ailment in his youth, a thing I found out by keeping my ears open and looking at a large photograph prominently displayed in her front room.

I turned to the next page in the old diary and it had in columns:

The Trips and The Trout Lost

April	7, 1891	Trout Lost	8
April	15, 1891	Trout Lost	6
April	23, 1891	Trout Lost	12
May	13, 1891	Trout Lost	9
May	23, 1891	Trout Lost	15
May	24, 1891	Trout Lost	10
May	25, 1891	Trout Lost	12
June	2, 1891	Trout Lost	18
June	6, 1891	Trout Lost	15
June	17, 1891	Trout Lost	7
June	19, 1891	Trout Lost	10
June	23, 1891	Trout Lost	14
July	4, 1891	Trout Lost	13
July	23, 1891	Trout Lost	11
August	10, 1891	Trout Lost	13
August	17, 1891	Trout Lost	8
August	20, 1891	Trout Lost	12
August	29, 1891	Trout Lost	21
September	3, 1891	Trout Lost	10
September	11, 1891	Trout Lost	7
September	19, 1891	Trout Lost	5
September	23, 1891	Trout Lost	3

Total Trips 22   Total Trout Lost 239

Average Number of Trout Lost Each Trip 10.8

I turned to the third page and it was just like the preceding page except the year was 1892 and Alonso Hagen went on 24 trips and lost 317 trout for an average of 13.2 trout lost each trip.

The next page was 1893 and the totals were 33 trips and 480 trout lost for an average of 14.5 trout lost each trip.

The next page was 1894. He went on 27 trips, lost 349 trout for an average of 12.9 trout lost each trip.

The next page was 1895. He went on 41 trips, lost 730 trout for an average of 17.8 trout lost each trip.

The next page was 1896. Alonso Hagen only went out 12

times and lost 115 trout for an average of 9.5 trout lost each trip.

The next page was 1897. He went on one trip and lost one trout for an average of one trout lost for one trip.

The last page of the diary was the grand totals for the years running from 1891–1897. Alonso Hagen went fishing 160 times and lost 2,231 trout for a seven-year average of 13.9 trout lost every time he went fishing.

Under the grand totals, there was a little Trout Fishing in America epitaph by Alonso Hagen. It said something like:

"I've had it.

I've gone fishing now for seven years

and I haven't caught a single trout.

I've lost every trout I ever hooked.

They either jump off

or twist off.

or squirm off

or break my leader

or flop off

or fuck off.

I have never even gotten my hands on a trout.

For all its frustration,

I believe it was an interesting experiment

in total loss

but next year somebody else

will have to go trout fishing.

Somebody else will have to go

out there."

THE TOWEL

We came down the road from Lake Josephus and down the road from Seafoam. We stopped along the way to get a drink of water. There was a small monument in the forest. I walked over to the monument to see what was happening. The glass door of the lookout was partly open and a towel was hanging on the other side.

At the center of the monument was a photograph. It was the classic forest lookout photograph I have seen before, from that America that existed during the 1920s and 30s.

There was a man in the photograph who looked a lot like Charles A. Lindbergh. He had that same <u>Spirit of St. Louis</u> nobility and purpose of expression, except that his North Atlantic was the forests of Idaho.

There was a woman cuddled up close to him. She was one of those great cuddly women of the past, wearing those pants they used to wear and those hightop, laced boots.

They were standing on the porch of the lookout. The sky was behind them, no more than a few feet away. People in those days liked to take that photograph and they liked to be in it.

There were words on the monument. They said:

> "In memory of Charley J. Langer, District
> Forest Ranger, Challis National Forest, Pilot
> Captain Bill Kelly and Co-Pilot Arthur A. Crofts,
> of the U.S. Army killed in an Airplane Crash
> April 5, 1943, near this point while searching
> for survivors of an Army Bomber Crew."

O it's far away now in the mountains that a photograph guards the memory of a man. The photograph is all alone out there. The snow is falling eighteen years after his death. It covers up the door. It covers up the towel.

SANDBOX MINUS JOHN
DILLINGER EQUALS WHAT?

Often I return to the cover of <u>Trout Fishing in America.</u> I
took the baby and went down there this morning. They were
watering the cover with big revolving sprinklers. I saw some
bread lying on the grass. It had been put there to feed the
pigeons.

The old Italians are always doing things like that. The
bread had been turned to paste by the water and was squashed
flat against the grass. Those dopey pigeons were waiting until
the water and grass had chewed up the bread for them, so
they wouldn't have to do it themselves.

I let the baby play in the sandbox and I sat down on a bench
and looked around. There was a beatnik sitting at the other
end of the bench. He had his sleeping bag beside him and he
was eating apple turnovers. He had a huge sack of apple turn-
overs and he was gobbling them down like a turkey. It was
probably a more valid protest than picketing missile bases.

The baby played in the sandbox. She had on a red dress
and the Catholic church was towering up behind her red dress.
There was a brick john between her dress and the church. It
was there by no accident. Ladies to the left and gents to the
right.

A red dress, I thought. Wasn't the woman who set John
Dillinger up for the FBI wearing a red dress? They called
her "The Woman in Red."

It seemed to me that was right. It was a red dress, but so
far, John Dillinger was nowhere in sight. My daughter
played alone in the sandbox.

Sandbox minus John Dillinger equals what?

The beatnik went and got a drink of water from the fountain
that was crucified on the wall of the brick john, more toward
the gents than the ladies. He had to wash all those apple turn-
overs down his throat.

There were three sprinklers going in the park. There was
one in front of the Benjamin Franklin statue and one to the
side of him and one just behind him. They were all turning in
circles. I saw Benjamin Franklin standing there patiently
through the water.

The sprinkler to the side of Benjamin Franklin hit the left-
hand tree. It sprayed hard against the trunk and knocked some
leaves down from the tree, and then it hit the center tree,
sprayed hard against the trunk and more leaves fell. Then it
sprayed against Benjamin Franklin, the water shot out to the
sides of the stone and a mist drifted down off the water. Ben-
jamin Franklin got his feet wet.

The sun was shining down hard on me. The sun was bright
and hot. After a while the sun made me think of my own dis-
comfort. The only shade fell on the beatnik.

The shade came down off the Lillie Hitchcock Coit statue
of some metal fireman saving a metal broad from a mental
fire. The beatnik now lay on the bench and the shade was two
feet longer than he was.

A friend of mine has written a poem about that statue. God-
damn, I wish he would write another poem about that statue,
so it would give me some shade two feet longer than my body.

I was right about "The Woman in Red," because ten min-
utes later they blasted John Dillinger down in the sandbox.
The sound of the machine-gun fire startled the pigeons and
they hurried on into the church.

My daughter was seen leaving in a huge black car shortly
after that. She couldn't talk yet, but that didn't make any dif-
ference. The red dress did it all.

John Dillinger's body lay half in and half out of the sand-
box, more toward the ladies than the gents. He was leaking
blood like those capsules we used to use with oleomargarine,
in those good old days when oleo was white like lard.

The huge black car pulled out and went up the street, bat-
light shining off the top. It stopped in front of the ice-cream
parlor at Filbert and Stockton.

An agent got out and went in and bought two hundred
double-decker ice-cream cones. He needed a wheelbarrow
to get them back to the car.

THE LAST TIME I SAW
TROUT FISHING IN AMERICA

The last time we met was in July on the Big Wood River, ten
miles away from Ketchum. It was just after Hemingway had
killed himself there, but I didn't know about his death at the
time. I didn't know about it until I got back to San Francisco
weeks after the thing had happened and picked up a copy of
Life magazine. There was a photograph of Hemingway on the
cover.

"I wonder what Hemingway's up to," I said to myself. I
looked inside the magazine and turned the pages to his death.
Trout Fishing in America forgot to tell me about it. I'm cer-
tain he knew. It must have slipped his mind.

The woman who travels with me had menstrual cramps.
She wanted to rest for a while, so I took the baby and my spin-
ning rod and went down to the Big Wood River. That's where
I met Trout Fishing in America.

I was casting a Super-Duper out into the river and letting
it swing down with the current and then ride on the water up
close to the shore. It fluttered there slowly and Trout Fish-
ing in America watched the baby while we talked.

I remember that he gave her some colored rocks to play
with. She liked him and climbed up onto his lap and she start-
ed putting the rocks in his shirt pocket.

We talked about Great Falls, Montana. I told Trout Fish-
ing in America about a winter I spent as a child in Great Falls.
"It was during the war and I saw a Deanna Durbin movie seven
times," I said.

The baby put a blue rock in Trout Fishing in America's
shirt pocket and he said, "I've been to Great Falls many
times. I remember Indians and fur traders. I remember
Lewis and Clark, but I don't remember ever seeing a Deanna
Durbin movie in Great Falls."

"I know what you mean," I said. "The other people in Great Falls did not share my enthusiasm for Deanna Durbin. The theater was always empty. There was a darkness to that theater different from any theater I've been in since. Maybe it was the snow outside and Deanna Durbin inside. I don't know what it was."

"What was the name of the movie?" Trout Fishing in America said.

"I don't know," I said. "She sang a lot. Maybe she was a chorus girl who wanted to go to college or she was a rich girl or they needed money for something or she did something. Whatever it was about, she sang! and sang! but I can't remember a God-damn word of it.

"One afternoon after I had seen the Deanna Durbin movie again, I went down to the Missouri River. Part of the Missouri was frozen over. There was a railroad bridge there. I was very relieved to see that the Missouri River had not changed and begun to look like Deanna Durbin.

"I'd had a childhood fancy that I would walk down to the Missouri River and it would look just like a Deanna Durbin movie—a chorus girl who wanted to go to college or she was a rich girl or they needed money for something or she did something.

"To this day I don't know why I saw that movie seven times. It was just as deadly as The Cabinet of Doctor Caligari. I wonder if the Missouri River is still there?" I said.

"It is," Trout Fishing in America said smiling. "But it doesn't look like Deanna Durbin."

The baby by this time had put a dozen or so of the colored rocks in Trout Fishing in America's shirt pocket. He looked at me and smiled and waited for me to go on about Great Falls, but just then I had a fair strike on my Super-Duper. I jerked the rod back and missed the fish.

Trout Fishing in America said, "I know that fish who just struck. You'll never catch him."

"Oh," I said.

"Forgive me," Trout Fishing in America said. "Go on ahead and try for him. He'll hit a couple of times more, but you won't catch him. He's not a particularly smart fish. Just lucky. Sometimes that's all you need."

"Yeah," I said. "You're right there."

I cast out again and continued talking about Great Falls.

90

Then in correct order I recited the twelve least important things ever said about Great Falls, Montana. For the twelfth and least important thing of all, I said, "Yeah, the telephone would ring in the morning. I'd get out of bed. I didn't have to answer the telephone. That had all been taken care of, years in advance.

"It would still be dark outside and the yellow wallpaper in the hotel room would be running back off the light bulb. I'd put my clothes on and go down to the restaurant where my stepfather cooked all night.

"I'd have breakfast, hot cakes, eggs and whatnot. Then he'd make my lunch for me and it would always be the same thing: a piece of pie and a stone-cold pork sandwich. Afterwards I'd walk to school. I mean the three of us, the Holy Trinity: me, a piece of pie, and a stone-cold pork sandwich. This went on for months.

"Fortunately it stopped one day without my having to do anything serious like grow up. We packed our stuff and left town on a bus. That was Great Falls, Montana. You say the Missouri River is still there?"

"Yes, but it doesn't look like Deanna Durbin," Trout Fishing in America said. "I remember the day Lewis discovered the falls. They left their camp at sunrise and a few hours later they came upon a beautiful plain and on the plain were more buffalo than they had ever seen before in one place.

"They kept on going until they heard the faraway sound of a waterfall and saw a distant column of spray rising and disappearing. They followed the sound as it got louder and louder. After a while the sound was tremendous and they were at the great falls of the Missouri River. It was about noon when they got there.

"A nice thing happened that afternoon, they went fishing below the falls and caught half a dozen trout, good ones, too, from sixteen to twenty-three inches long.

"That was June 13, 1805.

"No, I don't think Lewis would have understood it if the Missouri River had suddenly begun to look like a Deanna Durbin movie, like a chorus girl who wanted to go to college," Trout Fishing in America said.

IN THE CALIFORNIA BUSH

I've come home from Trout Fishing in America, the highway
bent its long smooth anchor about my neck and then stopped.
Now I live in this place. It took my whole life to get here, to
get to this strange cabin above Mill Valley.

We're staying with Pard and his girlfriend. They have
rented a cabin for three months, June 15th to September 15th,
for a hundred dollars. We are a funny bunch, all living here
together.

Pard was born of Okie parents in British Nigeria and came
to America when he was two years old and was raised as a
ranch kid in Oregon, Washington and Idaho.

He was a machine-gunner in the Second World War, against
the Germans. He fought in France and Germany. Sergeant
Pard. Then he came back from the war and went to some
hick college in Idaho.

After he graduated from college, he went to Paris and be-
came an Existentialist. He had a photograph taken of Exis-
tentialism and himself sitting at a sidewalk cafe. Pard was
wearing a beard and he looked as if he had a huge soul, with
barely enough room in his body to contain it.

When Pard came back to America from Paris, he worked
as a tugboat man on San Francisco Bay and as a railroad
man in the roundhouse at Filer, Idaho.

Of course, during this time he got married and had a kid.
The wife and kid are gone now, blown away like apples by the
fickle wind of the Twentieth Century. I guess the fickle wind
of all time. The family that fell in the autumn.

After he split up with his wife, he went to Arizona and was
a reporter and editor of newspapers. He honky-tonked in
Naco, a Mexican border town, drank Mescal Triunfo, played
cards and shot the roof of his house full of bullet holes.

Fard tells a story about waking one morning in Naco, all hungover, with the whips and jingles. A friend of his was sitting at the table with a bottle of whisky beside him.

Pard reached over and picked up a gun off a chair and took aim at the whisky bottle and fired. His friend was then sitting there, covered with flecks of glass, blood and whisky. "What the fuck you do that for?" he said.

Now in his late thirties Pard works at a print shop for $1.35 an hour. It is an avant-garde print shop. They print poetry and experimental prose. They pay him $1.35 an hour for operating a linotype machine. A $1.35 linotype operator is hard to find, outside of Hong Kong or Albania.

Sometimes when he goes down there, they don't even have enough lead for him. They buy their lead like soap, a bar or two at a time.

Pard's girlfriend is a Jew. Twenty-four years old, getting over a bad case of hepatitis, she kids Pard about a nude photograph of her that has the possibility of appearing in Playboy magazine.

"There's nothing to worry about," she says. "If they use that photograph, it only means that 12,000,000 men will look at my boobs."

This is all very funny to her. Her parents have money. As she sits in the other room in the California bush, she's on her father's payroll in New York.

What we eat is funny and what we drink is even more hilarious: turkeys, Gallo port, hot dogs, watermelons, Popeyes, salmon croquettes, frappes, Christian Brothers port, orange rye bread, canteloupes, Popeyes, salads, cheese—booze, grub and Popeyes.

Popeyes?

We read books like The Thief's Journal, Set This House on Fire, The Naked Lunch, Krafft-Ebing. We read Krafft-Ebing aloud all the time as if he were Kraft dinner.

"The mayor of a small town in Eastern Portugal was seen one morning pushing a wheelbarrow full of sex organs into the city hall. He was of tainted family. He had a woman's shoe in his back pocket. It had been there all night." Things like this make us laugh.

The woman who owns this cabin will come back in the autumn. She's spending the summer in Europe. When she comes back, she will spend only one day a week out here: Saturday.

She will never spend the night because she's afraid to. There is something here that makes her afraid.

Pard and his girlfriend sleep in the cabin and the baby sleeps in the basement, and we sleep outside, under the apple tree, waking at dawn to stare out across San Francisco Bay and then we go back to sleep again and wake once more, this time for a very strange thing to happen, and then we go back to sleep again after it has happened, and wake at sunrise to stare out across the bay.

Afterwards we go back to sleep again and the sun rises steadily hour after hour, staying in the branches of a eucalyptus tree just a ways down the hill, keeping us cool and asleep and in the shade. At last the sun pours over the top of the tree and then we have to get up, the hot sun upon us.

We go into the house and begin that two-hour yak-yak activity we call breakfast. We sit around and bring ourselves slowly back to consciousness, treating ourselves like fine pieces of china, and after we finish the last cup of the last cup of the last cup of coffee, it's time to think about lunch or go to the Goodwill in Fairfax.

So here we are, living in the California bush above Mill Valley. We could look right down on the main street of Mill Valley if it were not for the eucalyptus tree. We have to park the car a hundred yards away and come here along a tunnel-like path.

If all the Germans Pard killed during the war with his machine-gun were to come and stand in their uniforms around this place, it would make us pretty nervous.

There's the warm sweet smell of blackberry bushes along the path and in the late afternoon, quail gather around a dead unrequited tree that has fallen bridelike across the path. Sometimes I go down there and jump the quail. I just go down there to get them up off their butts. They're such beautiful birds. They set their wings and sail on down the hill.

O he was the one who was born to be king! That one, turning down through the Scotch broom and going over an upside-down car abandoned in the yellow grass. That one, his gray wings.

One morning last week, part way through the dawn, I awoke under the apple tree, to hear a dog barking and the rapid sound of hoofs coming toward me. The millennium? An invasion of Russians all wearing deer feet?

94

I opened my eyes and saw a deer running straight at me. It was a buck with large horns. There was a police dog chasing after it.

Arfwowfuck! Noisepoundpoundpoundpoundpoundpound! POUND! POUND!

The deer didn't swerve away. He just kept running straight at me, long after he had seen me, a second or two had passed.

Arfwowfuck! Noisepoundpoundpoundpoundpoundpound! POUND! POUND!

I could have reached out and touched him when he went by.

He ran around the house, circling the john, with the dog hot after him. They vanished over the hillside, leaving streamers of toilet paper behind them, flowing out and entangled through the bushes and vines.

Then along came the doe. She started up the same way, but not moving as fast. Maybe she had strawberries in her head.

"Whoa!" I shouted. "Enough is enough! I'm not selling newspapers!"

The doe stopped in her tracks, twenty-five feet away and turned and went down around the eucalyptus tree.

Well, that's how it's gone now for days and days. I wake up just before they come. I wake up for them in the same manner as I do for the dawn and the sunrise. Suddenly knowing they're on their way.

THE LAST MENTION OF TROUT
FISHING IN AMERICA SHORTY

Saturday was the first day of autumn and there was a festival
being held at the church of Saint Francis. It was a hot day
and the Ferris wheel was turning in the air like a thermo-
meter bent in a circle and given the grace of music.

But all this goes back to another time, to when my daught-
er was conceived. We'd just moved into a new apartment and
the lights hadn't been turned on yet. We were surrounded by
unpacked boxes of stuff and there was a candle burning like
milk on a saucer. So we got one in and we're sure it was the
right one.

A friend was sleeping in another room. In retrospect I
hope we didn't wake him up, though he has been awakened and
gone to sleep hundreds of times since then.

During the pregnancy I stared innocently at that growing
human center and had no idea the child therein contained
would ever meet Trout Fishing in America Shorty.

Saturday afternoon we went down to Washington Square.
We put the baby down on the grass and she took off running
toward Trout Fishing in America Shorty who was sitting un-
der the trees by the Benjamin Franklin statue.

He was on the ground leaning up against the right-hand
tree. There were some garlic sausages and some bread sit-
ting in his wheelchair as if it were a display counter in a
strange grocery store.

The baby ran down there and tried to make off with one of
his sausages.

Trout Fishing in America Shorty was instantly alerted,
then he saw it was a baby and relaxed. He tried to coax her
to come over and sit on his legless lap. She hid behind his
wheelchair, staring past the metal at him, one of her hands
holding onto a wheel.

"Come here, kid," he said. "Come over and see old Trout Fishing in America Shorty."

Just then the Benjamin Franklin statue turned green like a traffic light, and the baby noticed the sandbox at the other end of the park.

The sandbox suddenly looked better to her than Trout Fishing in America Shorty. She didn't care about his sausages any more either.

She decided to take advantage of the green light, and she crossed over to the sandbox.

Trout Fishing in America Shorty stared after her as if the space between them were a river growing larger and larger.

WITNESS FOR TROUT FISHING
IN AMERICA PEACE

In San Francisco around Easter time last year, they had a trout fishing in America peace parade. They had thousands of red stickers printed and they pasted them on their small foreign cars, and on means of national communication like telephone poles.

The stickers had WITNESS FOR TROUT FISHING IN AMERICA PEACE printed on them.

Then this group of college- and high-school-trained Communists, along with some Communist clergymen and their Marxist-taught children, marched to San Francisco from Sunnyvale, a Communist nerve center about forty miles away.

It took them four days to walk to San Francisco. They stopped overnight at various towns along the way, and slept on the lawns of fellow travelers.

They carried with them Communist trout fishing in America peace propaganda posters:

"DON'T DROP AN H-BOMB ON THE OLD FISHING HOLE!"

"ISAAC WALTON WOULD'VE HATED THE BOMB!"

"ROYAL COACHMAN, SI! ICBM, NO!"

They carried with them many other trout fishing in America peace inducements, all following the Communist world conquest line: the Gandhian nonviolence Trojan horse.

When these young, hard-core brainwashed members of the Communist conspiracy reached the "Panhandle," the emigre Oklahoma Communist sector of San Francisco, thousands of other Communists were waiting for them. These were Communists who couldn't walk very far. They barely had enough strength to make it downtown.

Thousands of Communists, protected by the police, marched

down to Union Square, located in the very heart of San Francisco. The Communist City Hall riots in 1960 had presented evidence of it, the police let hundreds of Communists escape, but the trout fishing in America peace parade was the final indictment: police protection.

Thousands of Communists marched right into the heart of San Francisco, and Communist speakers incited them for hours and the young people wanted to blow up Coit Tower, but the Communist clergy told them to put away their plastic bombs.

"Therefore all things whatsoever ye would that men should do to you, do ye even so to them . . . There will be no need for explosives," they said.

America needs no other proof. The Red shadow of the Gandhian nonviolence Trojan horse has fallen across America, and San Francisco is its stable.

Obsolete is the mad rapist's legendary piece of candy. At this very moment, Communist agents are handing out Witness for trout fishing in America peace tracts to innocent children riding the cable cars.

FOOTNOTE CHAPTER TO

"RED LIP"

Living in the California bush we had no garbage service. Our garbage was never greeted in the early morning by a man with a big smile on his face and a kind word or two. We couldn't burn any of the garbage because it was the dry season and everything was ready to catch on fire anyway, including ourselves. The garbage was a problem for a little while and then we discovered a way to get rid of it.

We took the garbage down to where there were three abandoned houses in a row. We carried sacks full of tin cans, papers, peelings, bottles and Popeyes.

We stopped at the last abandoned house where there were thousands of old receipts to the San Francisco <u>Chronicle</u> thrown all over the bed and the children's toothbrushes were still in the bathroom medicine cabinet.

Behind the place was an old outhouse and to get down to it, you had to follow the path down past some apple trees and a patch of strange plants that we thought were either a good spice that would certainly enhance our cooking or the plants were deadly nightshade that would cause our cooking to be less.

We carried the garbage down to the outhouse and always opened the door slowly because that was the only way you could open it, and on the wall there was a roll of toilet paper, so old it looked like a relative, perhaps a cousin, to the Magna Carta.

We lifted up the lid of the toilet and dropped the garbage down into the darkness. This went on for weeks and weeks until it became very funny to lift the lid of the toilet and instead of seeing darkness below or maybe the murky abstract outline of garbage, we saw bright, definite and lusty garbage heaped up almost to the top.

If you were a stranger and went down there to take an innocent crap, you would've had quite a surprise when you lifted up the lid.

We left the California bush just before it became necessary to stand on the toilet seat and step into that hole, crushing the garbage down like an accordion into the abyss.

THE CLEVELAND WRECKING

YARD

Until recently my knowledge about the Cleveland Wrecking
Yard had come from a couple of friends who'd bought things
there. One of them bought a huge window: the frame, glass
and everything for just a few dollars. It was a fine-looking
window.

Then he chopped a hole in the side of his house up on
Potrero Hill and put the window in. Now he has a panoramic
view of the San Francisco County Hospital.

He can practically look right down into the wards and see
old magazines eroded like the Grand Canyon from endless
readings. He can practically hear the patients thinking about
breakfast: I hate milk, and thinking about dinner: I hate peas,
and then he can watch the hospital slowly drown at night,
hopelessly entangled in huge bunches of brick seaweed.

He bought that window at the Cleveland Wrecking Yard.

My other friend bought an iron roof at the Cleveland Wreck-
ing Yard and took the roof down to Big Sur in an old station
wagon and then he carried the iron roof on his back up the
side of a mountain. He carried up half the roof on his back.
It was no picnic. Then he bought a mule, George, from Pleas-
anton. George carried up the other half of the roof.

The mule didn't like what was happening at all. He lost a
lot of weight because of the ticks, and the smell of the wild-
cats up on the plateau made him too nervous to graze there.
My friend said jokingly that George had lost around two hun-
dred pounds. The good wine country around Pleasanton in the
Livermore Valley probably had looked a lot better to George
than the wild side of the Santa Lucia Mountains.

My friend's place was a shack right beside a huge fire-
place where there had once been a great mansion during the
1920s, built by a famous movie actor. The mansion was built

before there was even a road down at Big Sur. The mansion had been brought over the mountains on the backs of mules, strung out like ants, bringing visions of the good life to the poison oak, the ticks, and the salmon.

The mansion was on a promontory, high over the Pacific. Money could see farther in the 1920s, and one could look out and see whales and the Hawaiian Islands and the Kuomintang in China.

The mansion burned down years ago.

The actor died.

His mules were made into soap.

His mistresses became bird nests of wrinkles.

Now only the fireplace remains as a sort of Carthaginian homage to Hollywood.

I was down there a few weeks ago to see my friend's roof. I wouldn't have passed up the chance for a million dollars, as they say. The roof looked like a colander to me. If that roof and the rain were running against each other at Bay Meadows, I'd bet on the rain and plan to spend my winnings at the World's Fair in Seattle.

My own experience with the Cleveland Wrecking Yard began two days ago when I heard about a used trout stream they had on sale out at the Yard. So I caught the Number 15 bus on Columbus Avenue and went out there for the first time.

There were two Negro boys sitting behind me on the bus. They were talking about Chubby Checker and the Twist. They thought that Chubby Checker was only fifteen years old because he didn't have a mustache. Then they talked about some other guy who did the twist forty-four hours in a row until he saw George Washington crossing the Delaware.

"Man, that's what I call twisting," one of the kids said.

"I don't think I could twist no forty-four hours in a row," the other kid said. "That's a lot of twisting."

I got off the bus right next to an abandoned Time Gasoline filling station and an abandoned fifty-cent self-service car wash. There was a long field on one side of the filling station. The field had once been covered with a housing project during the war, put there for the shipyard workers.

On the other side of the Time filling station was the Cleveland Wrecking Yard. I walked down there to have a look at the used trout stream. The Cleveland Wrecking Yard has a very long front window filled with signs and merchandise.

103

There was a sign in the window advertising a laundry marking machine for $65.00. The original cost of the machine was $175.00. Quite a saving.

There was another sign advertising new and used two and three ton hoists. I wondered how many hoists it would take to move a trout stream.

There was another sign that said:

THE FAMILY GIFT CENTER,
GIFT SUGGESTIONS FOR THE ENTIRE FAMILY

The window was filled with hundreds of items for the entire family. <u>Daddy, do you know what I want for Christmas? What, son? A bathroom. Mommy, do you know what I want for Christmas? What, Patricia? Some roofing material.</u>

There were jungle hammocks in the window for distant relatives and dollar-ten-cent gallons of earth-brown enamel paint for other loved ones.

There was also a big sign that said:

USED TROUT STREAM FOR SALE.
MUST BE SEEN TO BE APPRECIATED.

I went inside and looked at some ship's lanterns that were for sale next to the door. Then a salesman came up to me and said in a pleasant voice, "Can I help you?"

"Yes," I said. "I'm curious about the trout stream you have for sale. Can you tell me something about it? How are you selling it?"

"We're selling it by the foot length. You can buy as little as you want or you can buy all we've got left. A man came in here this morning and bought 563 feet. He's going to give it to his niece for a birthday present," the salesman said.

"We're selling the waterfalls separately of course, and the trees and birds, flowers, grass and ferns we're also selling extra. The insects we're giving away free with a minimum purchase of ten feet of stream."

"How much are you selling the stream for?" I asked.

"Six dollars and fifty-cents a foot," he said. "That's for the first hundred feet. After that it's five dollars a foot."

"How much are the birds?" I asked.

"Thirty-five cents apiece," he said. "But of course they're used. We can't guarantee anything."

"How wide is the stream?" I asked. "You said you were

selling it by the length, didn't you?"

"Yes," he said. "We're selling it by the length. Its width runs between five and eleven feet. You don't have to pay anything extra for width. It's not a big stream, but it's very pleasant."

"What kinds of animals do you have?" I asked.

"We only have three deer left," he said.

"Oh . . . What about flowers?"

"By the dozen," he said.

"Is the stream clear?" I asked.

"Sir," the salesman said. "I wouldn't want you to think that we would ever sell a murky trout stream here. We always make sure they're running crystal clear before we even think about moving them."

"Where did the stream come from?" I asked.

"Colorado," he said. "We moved it with loving care. We've never damaged a trout stream yet. We treat them all as if they were china."

"You're probably asked this all the time, but how's fishing in the stream?" I asked.

"Very good," he said. "Mostly German browns, but there are a few rainbows."

"What do the trout cost?" I asked.

"They come with the stream," he said. "Of course it's all luck. You never know how many you're going to get or how big they are. But the fishing's very good, you might say it's excellent. Both bait and dry fly," he said smiling.

"Where's the stream at?" I asked. "I'd like to take a look at it."

"It's around in back," he said. "You go straight through that door and then turn right until you're outside. It's stacked in lengths. You can't miss it. The waterfalls are upstairs in the used plumbing department."

"What about the animals?"

"Well, what's left of the animals are straight back from the stream. You'll see a bunch of our trucks parked on a road by the railroad tracks. Turn right on the road and follow it down past the piles of lumber. The animal shed's right at the end of the lot."

"Thanks," I said. "I think I'll look at the waterfalls first. You don't have to come with me. Just tell me how to get there and I'll find my own way."

105

"All right," he said. "Go up those stairs. You'll see a bunch of doors and windows, turn left and you'll find the used plumbing department. Here's my card if you need any help."

"Okay," I said. "You've been a great help already. Thanks a lot. I'll take a look around."

"Good luck," he said.

I went upstairs and there were thousands of doors there. I'd never seen so many doors before in my life. You could have built an entire city out of those doors. Doorstown. And there were enough windows up there to build a little suburb entirely out of windows. Windowville.

I turned left and went back and saw the faint glow of pearl-colored light. The light got stronger and stronger as I went farther back, and then I was in the used plumbing department, surrounded by hundreds of toilets.

The toilets were stacked on shelves. They were stacked five toilets high. There was a skylight above the toilets that made them glow like the Great Taboo Pearl of the South Sea movies.

Stacked over against the wall were the waterfalls. There were about a dozen of them, ranging from a drop of a few feet to a drop of ten or fifteen feet.

There was one waterfall that was over sixty feet long. There were tags on the pieces of the big falls describing the correct order for putting the falls back together again.

The waterfalls all had price tags on them. They were more expensive than the stream. The waterfalls were selling for $19.00 a foot.

I went into another room where there were piles of sweet-smelling lumber, glowing a soft yellow from a different color skylight above the lumber. In the shadows at the edge of the room under the sloping roof of the building were many sinks and urinals covered with dust, and there was also another waterfall about seventeen feet long, lying there in two lengths and already beginning to gather dust.

I had seen all I wanted of the waterfalls, and now I was very curious about the trout stream, so I followed the salesman's directions and ended up outside the building.

O I had never in my life seen anything like that trout stream. It was stacked in piles of various lengths: ten, fifteen, twenty feet, etc. There was one pile of hundred-foot

106

lengths. There was also a box of scraps. The scraps were
in odd sizes ranging from six inches to a couple of feet.

There was a loudspeaker on the side of the building and
soft music was coming out. It was a cloudy day and seagulls
were circling high overhead.

Behind the stream were big bundles of trees and bushes.
They were covered with sheets of patched canvas. You could
see the tops and roots sticking out the ends of the bundles.

I went up close and looked at the lengths of stream. I
could see some trout in them. I saw one good fish. I saw
some crawdads crawling around the rocks at the bottom.

It looked like a fine stream. I put my hand in the water.
It was cold and felt good.

I decided to go around to the side and look at the animals.
I saw where the trucks were parked beside the railroad
tracks. I followed the road down past the piles of lumber,
back to the shed where the animals were.

The salesman had been right. They were practically out
of animals. About the only thing they had left in any abun-
dance were mice. There were hundreds of mice.

Beside the shed was a huge wire birdcage, maybe fifty
feet high, filled with many kinds of birds. The top of the cage
had a piece of canvas over it, so the birds wouldn't get wet
when it rained. There were woodpeckers and wild canaries
and sparrows.

On my way back to where the trout stream was piled, I
found the insects. They were inside a prefabricated steel
building that was selling for eighty-cents a square foot. There
was a sign over the door. It said

INSECTS

A HALF-SUNDAY HOMAGE TO A
WHOLE LEONARDO DA VINCI

On this funky winter day in rainy San Francisco I've had a vision of Leonardo da Vinci. My woman's out slaving away, no day off, working on Sunday. She left here at eight o'clock this morning for Powell and California. I've been sitting here ever since like a toad on a log dreaming about Leonardo da Vinci.

I dreamt he was on the South Bend Tackle Company payroll, but of course, he was wearing different clothes and speaking with a different accent and possessor of a different childhood, perhaps an American childhood spent in a town like Lordsburg, New Mexico, or Winchester, Virginia.

I saw him inventing a new spinning lure for trout fishing in America. I saw him first of all working with his imagination, then with metal and color and hooks, trying a little of this and a little of that, and then adding motion and then taking it away and then coming back again with a different motion, and in the end the lure was invented.

He called his bosses in. They looked at the lure and all fainted. Alone, standing over their bodies, he held the lure in his hand and gave it a name. He called it "The Last Supper." Then he went about waking up his bosses.

In a matter of months that trout fishing lure was the sensation of the twentieth century, far outstripping such shallow accomplishments as Hiroshima or Mahatma Gandhi. Millions of "The Last Supper" were sold in America. The Vatican ordered ten thousand and they didn't even have any trout there.

Testimonials poured in. Thirty-four ex-presidents of the United States all said, "I caught my limit on 'The Last Supper.'"

TROUT FISHING IN AMERICA

NIB

He went up to Chemault, that's in Eastern Oregon, to cut
Christmas trees. He was working for a very small enter-
prise. He cut the trees, did the cooking and slept on the
kitchen floor. It was cold and there was snow on the ground.
The floor was hard. Somewhere along the line, he found an
old Air Force flight jacket. That was a big help in the cold.

The only woman he could find up there was a three-hundred-
pound Indian squaw. She had twin fifteen-year-old daughters
and he wanted to get into them. But the squaw worked it so
he only got into her. She was clever that way.

The people he was working for wouldn't pay him up there.
They said he'd get it all in one sum when they got back to
San Francisco. He'd taken the job because he was broke,
really broke.

He waited and cut trees in the snow, laid the squaw,
cooked bad food—they were on a tight budget—and he
washed the dishes. Afterwards, he slept on the kitchen floor
in his Air Force flight jacket.

When they finally got back to town with the trees, those
guys didn't have any money to pay him off. He had to wait
around the lot in Oakland until they sold enough trees to pay
him off.

"Here's a lovely tree, ma'am."

"How much?"

"Ten dollars."

"That's too much."

"I have a lovely two-dollar tree here, ma'am. Actually,
it's only half a tree, but you can stand it up right next to a
wall and it'll look great, ma'am."

"I'll take it. I can put it right next to my weather clock.
This tree is the same color as the queen's dress. I'll take it.

You said two dollars?"

"That's right, ma'am."

"Hello, sir. Yes . . . Uh-huh . . . Yes . . . You say that you want to bury your aunt with a Christmas tree in her coffin? Uh-huh . . . She wanted it that way . . . I'll see what I can do for you, sir. Oh, you have the measurements of the coffin with you? Very good . . . We have our coffin-sized Christmas trees right over here, sir."

Finally he was paid off and he came over to San Francisco and had a good meal, a steak dinner at Le Boeuf and some good booze, Jack Daniels, and then went out to the Fillmore and picked up a good-looking, young, Negro whore, and he got laid in the Albert Bacon Fall Hotel.

The next day he went down to a fancy stationery store on Market Street and bought himself a thirty-dollar fountain pen, one with a gold nib.

He showed it to me and said, "Write with this, but don't write hard because this pen has got a gold nib, and a gold nib is very impressionable. After a while it takes on the personality of the writer. Nobody else can write with it. This pen becomes just like a person's shadow. It's the only pen to have. But be careful."

I thought to myself what a lovely nib trout fishing in America would make with a stroke of cool green trees along the river's shore, wild flowers and dark fins pressed against the paper.

PRELUDE TO THE
MAYONNAISE CHAPTER

"The Eskimos live among ice all their lives but have no single word for ice." —Man: His First Million Years, by M. F. Ashley Montagu

"Human language is in some ways similar to, but in other ways vastly different from, other kinds of animal communication. We simply have no idea about its evolutionary history, though many people have speculated about its possible origins. There is, for instance, the 'bow-bow' theory, that language started from attempts to imitate animal sounds. Or the 'ding-dong' theory, that it arose from natural sound-producing responses. Or the 'pooh-pooh' theory, that it began with violent outcries and exclamations . . . We have no way of knowing whether the kinds of men represented by the earliest fossils could talk or not . . . Language does not leave fossils, at least not until it has become written . . ." —Man in Nature, by Marston Bates

"But no animal up a tree can initiate a culture." —"The Simian Basis of Human Mechanics," in Twilight of Man, by Earnest Albert Hooton

Expressing a human need, I always wanted to write a book that ended with the word Mayonnaise.

THE MAYONNAISE CHAPTER

Feb 3-1952

Dearest Florence and Harv.

I just heard from Edith about
the passing of Mr. Good. Our heart
goes out to you in deepest sympathy
Gods will be done. He has lived a
good long life and he has gone to
a better place. You were expecting
it and it was nice you could see
him yesterday even if he did not
know you. You have our prayers
and love and we will see you soon.
God bless you both.

Love Mother and Nancy.

P.S.
Sorry I forgot to give you the mayonaise.

Writing 20

RICHARD BRAUTIGAN

The Pill
versus
The Springhill Mine
Disaster

This book is for Miss Marcia Pacaud of Montreal, Canada.

Contents

The Pill *versus* the Springhill Mine Disaster

All Watched Over by Machines of Loving Grace

I like to think (and
the sooner the better!)
of a cybernetic meadow
where mammals and computers
live together in mutually
programming harmony
like pure water
touching clear sky.

I like to think
   (right now, please!)
of a cybernetic forest
filled with pines and electronics
where deer stroll peacefully
past computers
as if they were flowers
with spinning blossoms.

I like to think
   (it has to be!)
of a cybernetic ecology
where we are free of our labors
and joined back to nature,
returned to our mammal
brothers and sisters,
and all watched over
by machines of loving grace.

Horse Child Breakfast

Horse child breakfast,
what are you doing to me?
with your long blonde legs?
with your long blonde face?
with your long blonde hair?
with your perfect blonde ass?

I swear I'll never be the
   same again!

Horse child breakfast,
what you're doing to me,
I want done forever.

General Custer Versus the Titanic

For the soldiers of the Seventh Cavalry who were killed at the Little Bighorn River and the passengers who were lost on the maiden voyage of the Titanic.
God bless their souls.

Yes! it's true all my visions
have come home to roost at last.
They are all true now and stand
around me like a bouquet of
lost ships and doomed generals.
I gently put them away in a
beautiful and disappearing vase.

The Beautiful Poem

I go to bed in Los Angeles thinking
   about you.

Pissing a few moments ago
I looked down at my penis
   affectionately.

Knowing it has been inside
you twice today makes me
   feel beautiful.

                    3 A.M
                    January 15, 1967

4

Private Eye Lettuce

Three crates of Private Eye Lettuce,
the name and drawing of a detective
with magnifying glass on the sides
of the crates of lettuce,
form a great cross in man's imagination
and his desire to name
the objects of this world.
I think I'll call this place Golgotha
and have some salad for dinner.

A Boat

O beautiful
was the werewolf
in his evil forest.
We took him
to the carnival
and he started
  crying
when he saw
the Ferris wheel.
Electric
green and red tears
flowed down
his furry cheeks.
He looked
like a boat
out on the dark
water.

The Shenevertakesherwatchoff Poem

Because you always have a clock
strapped to your body, it's natural
that I should think of you as the
   correct time:
with your long blonde hair at 8:03,
and your pulse-lightning breasts at
11:17, and your rose-meow smile at 5:30,
   I know I'm right.

Karma Repair Kit: Items 1-4

1. Get enough food to eat,
    and eat it.

2. Find a place to sleep where it is quiet,
    and sleep there.

3. Reduce intellectual and emotional noise
    until you arrive at the silence of yourself,
    and listen to it.

4.

Oranges

Oh, how perfect death
computes an orange wind
that glows from your footsteps,

and you stop to die in
an orchard where the harvest
fills the stars.

San Francisco

This poem was found written on a paper bag by Richard Brautigan in a laundromat in San Francisco. The author is unknown.

By accident, you put
Your money in my
Machine (#4)
By accident, I put
My money in another
Machine (#6)
On purpose, I put
Your clothes in the
Empty machine full
Of water and no
Clothes

It was lonely.

Xerox Candy Bar

Ah,
you're just a copy
of all the candy bars
I've ever eaten.

Discovery

The petals of the vagina unfold
like Christopher Columbus
taking off his shoes.

Is there anything more beautiful
than the bow of a ship
touching a new world?

Widow's Lament

It's not quite cold enough
to go borrow some firewood
from the neighbors.

The Pomegranate Circus

I am desolate in dimension
circling the sky
                    like a rainy bird,

wet from toe to crown
wet from bill to wing.

I feel like a drowned king
at the pomegranate circus.

I vowed last year
that I wouldn't go again
but here I sit in my usual seat,
   dripping and clapping

as the pomegranates go by
in their metallic costumes.

December 25, 1966

The Winos on Potrero Hill

Alas, they get
their bottles
from a small
neighborhood store.
The old Russian
sells them port
and passes no moral
judgment.   They go
and sit under
the green bushes
that grow along
the wooden stairs.
They could almost
be exotic flowers,
they drink so
quietly.

The First Winter Snow

Oh, pretty girl, you have trapped
yourself in the wrong body.   Twenty
extra pounds hang like a lumpy
tapestry on your perfect mammal nature.

Three months ago you were like a
deer staring at the first winter snow.

Now Aphrodite thumbs her nose at you
and tells stories behind your back.

Death Is a Beautiful Car Parked Only

for Emmett

Death is a beautiful car parked only
to be stolen on a street lined with trees
whose branches are like the intestines
    of an emerald.

You hotwire death, get in, and drive away
like a flag made from a thousand burning
    funeral parlors.

You have stolen death because you're bored.
There's nothing good playing at the movies
    in San Francisco.

You joyride around for a while listening
to the radio, and then abandon death, walk
away, and leave death for the police
    to find.

Surprise

I lift the toilet seat
   as if it were the nest of a bird
and I see cat tracks
   all around the edge of the bowl.

Your Departure Versus the Hindenburg

Every time we say good-bye
I see it as an extension of
    the Hindenburg:
that great 1937 airship exploding
in medieval flames like a burning castle
    above New Jersey.
When you leave the house, the
shadow of the Hindenburg enters
    to take your place.

Education

There is a woman
on the Klamath River
who has five
hundred children
in the basement,
stuffed like
hornets into
a mud nest.
Great Sparrow
is their father.
Once a day
he pulls a
red wagon between
them and
that's all
they know.

Love Poem

It's so nice
to wake up in the morning
   all alone
and not have to tell somebody
   you love them
when you don't love them
   any more.

The Fever Monument

I walked across the park to the fever monument.
It was in the center of a glass square surrounded
by red flowers and fountains. The monument
was in the shape of a sea horse and the plaque read
We got hot and died.

At the California Institute of Technology

I don't care how God-damn smart
these guys are: I'm bored.

It's been raining like hell all day long
and there's nothing to do.

> *Written January 24, 1967*
> *while poet-in-residence at*
> *the California Institute of*
> *Technology.*

A Lady

Her face grips at her mouth
like a leaf to a tree
or a tire to a highway
or a spoon to a bowl of soup.

She just can't let go
   with a smile,
   the poor dear.

No matter what happens
her face is always a maple tree
   Highway 101
   tomato.

"Star-Spangled" Nails

You've got
some "Star-Spangled"
   nails
in your coffin, kid.
That's what
they've done for you,
   son.

The Pumpkin Tide

I saw thousands of pumpkins last night
come floating in on the tide,
bumping up against the rocks and
rolling up on the beaches;
it must be Halloween in the sea.

Adrenalin Mother

Adrenalin Mother,
with your dress of comets
and shoes of swift bird wings
and shadow of jumping fish,
thank you for touching,
understanding and loving my life.
Without you, I am dead.

The Wheel

The wheel: it's a thing like pears
rotting under a tree in August.
O golden wilderness!
The bees travel in covered wagons
and the Indians hide in the heat.

Map Shower

For Marcia

I want your hair
to cover me with maps
of new places,

so everywhere I go
will be as beautiful
as your hair.

29

A Postcard from Chinatown

The Chinese smoke opium
in their bathrooms.
They all get in the bathroom
and lock the door.
The old people sit in the tub
and the children sit
on the floor.

The Double-Bed Dream Gallows

Driving through
hot brushy country
in the late autumn,
I saw a hawk
crucified on a
barbed-wire fence.

I guess as a kind
of advertisement
to other hawks,
saying from the pages
of a leading women's
  magazine,

"She's beautiful,
but burn all the maps
to your body.
I'm not here
of my own choosing."

December 30

At 1:03 in the morning a fart
smells like a marriage between
an avocado and a fish head.

I have to get out of bed
to write this down without
    my glasses on.

The Sawmill

I am the sawmill
abandoned even by the ghosts
in the middle of a pasture.
   Opera!
    Opera!
The horses won't go near
my God-damn thing.
They stay over by the creek.

The Way She Looks at It

Every time I see him, I think:
Gee, am I glad he's not
   my old man.

Yes, the Fish Music

A trout-colored wind blows
through my eyes, through my fingers,
and I remember how the trout
used to hide from the dinosaurs
when they came to drink at the river.
The trout hid in subways, castles
and automobiles.   They waited patiently
for the dinosaurs to go away.

The Chinese Checker Players

When I was six years old
I played Chinese checkers
    with a woman
who was ninety-three years old.
She lived by herself
in an apartment down the hall
    from ours.
We played Chinese checkers
every Monday and Thursday nights.
While we played she usually talked
about her husband
who had been dead for seventy years,
and we drank tea and ate cookies
    and cheated.

I've Never Had It Done so Gently Before

For M

The sweet juices of your mouth
are like castles bathed in honey.
I've never had it done so gently before.
You have put a circle of castles
around my penis and you swirl them
like sunlight on the wings of birds.

Our Beautiful West Coast Thing

We are a coast people
There is nothing but ocean out beyond us.
— Jack Spicer

I sit here dreaming
long thoughts of California

at the end of a November day
below a cloudy twilight
   near the Pacific

listening to The Mamas and The Papas
   THEY'RE GREAT

singing a song about breaking
somebody's heart and digging it!

I think I'll get up
and dance around the room.

   Here I go!

Man

With his hat on
he's about five inches taller
than a taxicab.

The Silver Stairs of Ketchikan

2 A.M. is the best time
to climb the silver stairs
of Ketchikan and go up into the trees
and the dark prowling deer.

When my wife gets out of bed
to feed the baby at 2 A.M., she turns
on all the lights in Ketchikan
and people start banging on the doors
and swearing at one another.

That's the best time
to climb the silver stairs
of Ketchikan and go up into the trees
and the dark prowling deer.

Hollywood

January 26, 1967
at 3:15 in the afternoon

Sitting here in Los Angeles
parked on a rundown residential
   back street,
staring up at the word
   HOLLYWOOD
written on some lonely mountains,
I'm listening very carefully
to rock and roll radio
   (Lovin' Spoonful)
   (Jefferson Airplane)
while people are slowly
putting out their garbage cans.

Your Necklace Is Leaking

For Marcia

Your necklace is leaking
and blue light drips
from your beads to cover
your beautiful breasts
with a clear African dawn.

Haiku Ambulance

A piece of green pepper
  fell
off the wooden salad bowl:
  so what?

It's Going Down

Magic is the color of the thing you wear
with a dragon for a button
and a lion for a lamp
with a carrot for a collar
and a salmon for a zipper.

> Hey!   You're turning me on: baby.
> That's the way it's going down.
>
> WOW!

Alas, Measured Perfectly

Saturday, August 25, 1888.   5:20 P.M.
is the name of a photograph of two
old women in a front yard, beside
a white house.   One of the women is
sitting in a chair with a dog in her
lap.   The other woman is looking at
some flowers.   Perhaps the women are
happy, but then it is Saturday, August
25, 1888.   5:21 P.M., and all over.

Hey, Bacon!

The moon like:
mischievous bacon
crisps its desire

   (while)

I harbor myself
toward two eggs
over easy.

The Rape of Ophelia

Her clothes spread wide and mermaid-like awhile
they bore her up: which time she chanted snatches
of old tunes, and sweet Ophelia floated down the river
past black stones until she came to an evil fisherman
who was dressed in clothes that had no childhood,
and beautiful Ophelia floated like an April church
into his shadow, and he, the evil fisherman of our dreams,
waded out into the river and captured the poor mad girl,
and taking her into the deep grass, he killed her
with the shock of his body, and he placed her back
into the river, and Laertes said, Alas, then she is drown'd!
Too much of water hast thou, poor Ophelia.

A CandleLion Poem

For Michael

Turn a candle inside out
and you've got the smallest
portion of a lion standing
there at the edge of the
    shadows.

I Feel Horrible. She Doesn't

I feel horrible.   She doesn't
love me and I wander around
the house like a sewing machine
that's just finished sewing
a turd to a garbage can lid.

Cyclops

A glass of lemonade
travels across this world
like the eye of the cyclops

If a child doesn't drink
the lemonade,
    Ulysses will.

Flowers for Those You Love

Butcher, baker, candlestick maker,
anybody can get VD,
including those you love.

Please see a doctor
if you think you've got it.

You'll feel better afterwards
and so will those you love.

THE GALILEE HITCH-HIKER

The Galilee Hitch-Hiker
Part 1

Baudelaire was
driving a Model A
across Galilee.
He picked up a
hitch-hiker named
Jesus who had
been standing among
a school of fish,
feeding them
pieces of bread.
"Where are you
going?" asked
Jesus, getting
into the front
seat.
"Anywhere, anywhere
out of this world!"
shouted
Baudelaire.
"I'll go with you
as far as
Golgotha,"
said Jesus.
"I have a
concession
at the carnival
there, and I
must not be
late."

The American Hotel
Part 2

Baudelaire was sitting
in a doorway with a wino
on San Francisco's skidrow.
The wino was a million
years old and could remember
   dinosaurs.
Baudelaire and the wino
were drinking Petri Muscatel.
"One must always be drunk,"
   said Baudelaire.
"I live in the American Hotel,"
said the wino.   "And I can
   remember dinosaurs."
"Be you drunken ceaselessly,"
   said Baudelaire.

1939
Part 3

Baudelaire used to come
to our house and watch
me grind coffee.
That was in 1939
and we lived in the slums
of Tacoma.
My mother would put
the coffee beans in the grinder.
I was a child
and would turn the handle,
pretending that it was
   a hurdy-gurdy,
and Baudelaire would pretend
that he was a monkey,
hopping up and down
and holding out
a tin cup.

The Flowerburgers
Part 4

Baudelaire opened
up a hamburger stand
in San Francisco,
but he put flowers
between the buns.
People would come in
and say, "Give me a
hamburger with plenty
of onions on it."
Baudelaire would give
them a flowerburger
instead and the people
would say, "What kind
of a hamburger stand
is this?"

The Hour of Eternity
Part 5

"The Chinese
read the time
in the eyes
of cats,"
said Baudelaire
and went into
a jewelry store
on Market Street.
He came out
a few moments
later carrying
a twenty-one
jewel Siamese
cat that he
wore on the
end of a
golden chain.

Salvador Dali
Part 6

"Are you
or aren't you
going to eat
your soup,
you bloody old
cloud merchant?"
Jeanne Duval
shouted,
hitting Baudelaire
on the back
as he sat
daydreaming
out the window.
Baudelaire was
startled.
Then he laughed
like hell,
waving his spoon
in the air
like a wand
changing the room
into a painting
by Salvador
Dali, changing
the room
into a painting
by Van Gogh.

A Baseball Game
Part 7

Baudelaire went
to a baseball game
and bought a hot dog
and lit up a pipe
of opium.
The New York Yankees
were playing
the Detroit Tigers.
In the fourth inning
an angel committed
suicide by jumping
off a low cloud.
The angel landed
on second base,
causing the
whole infield
to crack like
a huge mirror.
The game was
called on
account of
fear.

Insane Asylum
Part 8

Baudelaire went
to the insane asylum
disguised as a
psychiatrist.
He stayed there
for two months
and when he left,
the insane asylum
loved him so much
that it followed
him all over
California,
and Baudelaire
laughed when the
insane asylum
rubbed itself
up against his
leg like a
strange cat.

My Insect Funeral
Part 9

When I was a child
I had a graveyard
where I buried insects
and dead birds under
a rose tree.
I would bury the insects
in tin foil and match boxes.
I would bury the birds
in pieces of red cloth.
It was all very sad
and I would cry
as I scooped the dirt
into their small graves
with a spoon.
Baudelaire would come
and join in
my insect funerals,
saying little prayers
the size of
dead birds.

San Francisco
February 1958

It's Raining in Love

I don't know what it is,
but I distrust myself
when I start to like a girl
    a lot.

It makes me nervous.
I don't say the right things
or perhaps I start
    to examine,
                evaluate,
                        compute
    what I am saying.

If I say, "Do you think it's going to rain?"
and she says, "I don't know,"
I start thinking: Does she really like me?

In other words
I get a little creepy.

A friend of mine once said,
"It's twenty times better to be friends
    with someone
than it is to be in love with them."

I think he's right and besides,
it's raining somewhere, programming flowers
and keeping snails happy.
    That's all taken care of.

            BUT
if a girl likes me a lot
and starts getting real nervous
and suddenly begins asking me funny questions

and looks sad if I give the wrong answers
and she says things like,
"Do you think it's going to rain?"
and I say, "It beats me,"
and she says, "Oh,"
and looks a little sad
at the clear blue California sky,
I think:　Thank God, it's you, baby, this time
　　instead of me.

Poker Star

It's a star that looks
like a poker game above
the mountains of eastern
   Oregon.
There are three men playing.
They are all sheepherders.
One of them has two pair,
the others have nothing.

To England

There are no postage stamps that send letters
back to England three centuries ago,
no postage stamps that make letters
travel back until the grave hasn't been dug yet,
and John Donne stands looking out the window,
it is just beginning to rain this April morning,
and the birds are falling into the trees
like chess pieces into an unplayed game,
and John Donne sees the postman coming up the street,
the postman walks very carefully because his cane
is made of glass.

I Lie Here in a Strange Girl's Apartment

For Marcia

I lie here in a strange girl's apartment.
She has poison oak, a bad sunburn
   and is unhappy.
She moves about the place
like distant gestures of solemn glass.

She opens and closes things.
She turns the water on,
and she turns the water off.

All the sounds she makes are faraway.
They could be in a different city.
It is dusk and people are staring
out the windows of that city.
Their eyes are filled with the sounds
   of what she is doing.

Hey!   This Is What It's All About

For Jeff Sheppard

No publication
No money
No star
No fuck
_____

   A friend came over to the house
a few days ago and read one of my poems.
He came back today and asked to read the
same poem over again.   After he finished
reading it, he said, "It makes me want
   to write poetry."

My Nose Is Growing Old

Yup.
A long lazy September look
in the mirror
say it's true:

I'm 31
and my nose is growing
    old.

It starts about $1/2$
    an inch
below the bridge
and strolls geriatrically
    down
for another inch or so:
    stopping.

Fortunately, the rest
of the nose is comparatively
    young.

I wonder if girls
will want me with an
    old nose.

I can hear them now
the heartless bitches!

"He's cute
            but his nose
is old."

Crab Cigar

I was watching a lot of crabs
eating in the tide pools
of the Pacific a few days ago.

When I say a lot: I mean
hundreds of crabs.   They eat
  like cigars.

The Sidney Greenstreet Blues

I think something beautiful
and amusing is gained
by remembering Sidney Greenstreet,
but it is a fragile thing.

The hand picks up a glass.
The eye looks at the glass
and then hand, glass and eye
    fall away.

Comets

There are comets
that flash through
our mouths wearing
the grace
of oceans and galaxies.

God knows,
we try to do the best
we can.

There are comets
connected to chemicals
that telescope
down our tongues
to burn out against
the air.

I know
we do.

There are comets
that laugh at us
from behind our teeth
wearing the clothes
of fish and birds.

We try.

I Live in the Twentieth Century

For Marcia

I live in the Twentieth Century
and you lie here beside me.   You
were unhappy when you fell asleep.
There was nothing I could do about
it.   I felt helpless.   Your face
is so beautiful that I cannot stop
to describe it, and there's nothing
I can do to make you happy while
   you sleep.

The Castle of the Cormorants

Hamlet with
a cormorant
under his arm
married Ophelia.
She was still
wet from drowning.
She looked like
a white flower
that had been
left in the
rain too long.
I love you,
said Ophelia,
and I love
that dark
bird you
hold in
your arms.

Big Sur
February 1958

Lovers

I changed her bedroom:
raised the ceiling four feet,
removed all of her things
(and the clutter of her life)
painted the walls white,
placed a fantastic calm
   in the room,
a silence that almost had a scent,
put her in a low brass bed
with white satin covers,
and I stood there in the doorway
watching her sleep, curled up,
with her face turned away
   from me.

Sonnet

The sea is like
an old nature poet
who died of a
heart attack in a
public latrine.
His ghost still
haunts the urinals.
At night he can
be heard walking
around barefooted
in the dark.
Somebody stole
his shoes.

Indirect Popcorn

What a good time fancy!
like a leisure white interior
with long yellow curtains.
I'll take it to sleep with me tonight
and hope that my dreams are built
toward beautiful blonde women eating
    indirect popcorn.

Star Hole

I sit here
on the perfect end
of a star,

watching light
pour itself toward
    me.

The light pours
itself through
a small hole
in the sky.

I'm not very happy,
but I can see
how things are
    faraway.

Albion Breakfast

For Susan

Last night (here) a long pretty girl
asked me to write a poem about Albion,
so she could put it in a black folder
that has albion printed nicely
    in white on the cover.

I said yes.   She's at the store now
getting something for breakfast.
I'll surprise her with this poem
    when she gets back.

Let's Voyage into the New American House

There are doors
that want to be free
from their hinges to
fly with perfect clouds.

There are windows
that want to be
released from their
frames to run with
the deer through
back country meadows.

There are walls
that want to prowl
with the mountains
through the early
morning dusk.

There are floors
that want to digest
their furniture into
flowers and trees.

There are roofs
that want to travel
gracefully with
the stars through
circles of darkness.

November 3

I'm sitting in a cafe,
drinking a Coke.

A fly is sleeping
on a paper napkin.

I have to wake him up,
so I can wipe my glasses.

There's a pretty girl
I want to look at.

The Postman

The smell
> of vegetables
>> on a cold day
performs faithfully an act of reality
like a knight in search of the holy grail
or a postman on a rural route looking
for a farm that isn't there.
  Carrots, peppers and berries.
  Nerval, Baudelaire and Rimbaud.

A Mid-February Sky Dance

Dance toward me, please, as
if you were a star
with light-years piled
on top of your hair,
  smiling,

and I will dance toward you
as if I were darkness
with bats piled like a hat
  on top of my head.

The Quail

There are three quail in a cage next door,
and they are the sweet delight of our mornings,
calling to us like small frosted cakes:
    bobwhitebobwhitebobwhite,
but at night they drive our God-damn cat Jake crazy.
They run around that cage like pinballs
as he stands out there,
smelling their asses through the wire.

1942

Piano tree, play
in the dark concert halls
of my uncle,
twenty-six years old, dead
and homeward bound
on a ship from Sitka,
his coffin travels
like the fingers
of Beethoven
over a glass
of wine.

Piano tree, play
in the dark concert halls
of my uncle,
a legend of my childhood, dead,
they send him back
to Tacoma.
At night his coffin
travels like the birds
that fly beneath the sea,
never touching the sky.

Piano tree, play
in the dark concert halls
of my uncle,
take his heart
for a lover
and take his death
for a bed,
and send him homeward bound
on a ship from Sitka
to bury him
where I was born.

Milk for the Duck

ZAP!
unlaid / 20 days

my sexual image
isn't worth a shit.

If I were dead
I couldn't attract
a female fly.

The Return of the Rivers

All the rivers run into the sea;
yet the sea is not full;
unto the place from whence the rivers come,
thither they return again.

It is raining today
in the mountains.

It is a warm green rain
with love
in its pockets
for spring is here,
and does not dream
of death.

Birds happen music
like clocks ticking heavens
in a land
where children love spiders,
and let them sleep
in their hair.

A slow rain sizzles
on the river
like a pan
full of frying flowers,
and with each drop
of rain
the ocean
begins again.

A Good-Talking Candle

I had a good-talking candle
last night in my bedroom.

I was very tired but I wanted
somebody to be with me,
    so I lit a candle

and listened to its comfortable
voice of light until I was asleep.

The Horse That Had a Flat Tire

Once upon a valley
there came down
from some goldenblue mountains
a handsome young prince
who was riding
a dawncolored horse
named Lordsburg.

   I love you
   You're my breathing castle
   Gentle so gentle
   We'll live forever

In the valley
there was a beautiful maiden
whom the prince
drifted into love with
like a New Mexico made from
apple thunder and long
glass beds.

   I love you
   You're my breathing castle
   Gentle so gentle
   We'll live forever

The prince enchanted
the maiden
and they rode off
on the dawncolored horse
named Lordsburg
toward the goldenblue mountains.

I love you
You're my breathing castle
Gentle so gentle
We'll live forever

They would have lived
happily ever after
if the horse hadn't had
a flat tire
in front of a dragon's
house.

Kafka's Hat

With the rain falling
surgically against the roof,
I ate a dish of ice cream
that looked like Kafka's hat.

It was a dish of ice cream
tasting like an operating table
with the patient staring
up at the ceiling.

Nine Things

It's night

and a numbered beauty
lapses at the wind,

chortles with the
branches of a tree,

  giggles,

plays shadow dance
with a dead kite,

cajoles affection
from falling leaves,

and knows four
other things.

One is the color
of your hair.

Linear Farewell, Nonlinear Farewell

When he went out the door,
he said he wasn't coming back,
but he came back, the son-
ofabitch, and now I'm pregnant,
and he won't get off his ass.

Mating Saliva

A girl in a green mini-
skirt, not very pretty, walks
   down the street.

A businessman stops, turns
to stare at her ass
that looks like a moldy
   refrigerator.

There are now 200,000,000 people
   in America.

Sit Comma and Creeley Comma

It's spring and the nun
like a black frog
builds her tarpaper shack
beside the lake.
How beautiful she is
(and looks) surrounded
by her rolls of tarpaper.
They know her name
and they speak her name.

Automatic Anthole

Driven by hunger, I had another
forced bachelor dinner tonight.
I had a lot of trouble making
up my mind whether to eat Chinese
food or have a hamburger.   God,
I hate eating dinner alone.   It's
   like being dead.

The Symbol

When I was hitch-hiking down to Big Sur,
Moby Dick stopped and picked me up.   He was driving
a truckload of sea gulls to San Luis Obispo.

"Do you like being a truckdriver better than you
do a whale?" I asked.

"Yeah," Moby Dick said.   "Hoffa is a lot better
to us whales than Captain Ahab ever was.

The old fart."

I Cannot Answer You Tonight in Small Portions

I cannot answer you tonight in small portions.
Torn apart by stormy love's gate, I float
like a phantom facedown in a well where
the cold dark water reflects vague half-built
                stars
and trades all our affection, touching, sleeping
together for tribunal distance standing like
a drowned train just beyond a pile of Eskimo
                skeletons.

Your Catfish Friend

If I were to live my life
in catfish forms
in scaffolds of skin and whiskers
at the bottom of a pond
and you were to come by
    one evening
when the moon was shining
down into my dark home
and stand there at the edge
    of my affection
and think, "It's beautiful
here by this pond.   I wish
    somebody loved me,"
I'd love you and be your catfish
friend and drive such lonely
thoughts from your mind
and suddenly you would be
    at peace,
and ask yourself, "I wonder
if there are any catfish
in this pond?   It seems like
a perfect place for them."

December 24

She's mending the rain with her hair.
She's turning the darkness on.
   Glue / switch!
That's all I have to report.

Horse Race

July 19, a dog has been run over by an airplane,
an act that brings into this world the energy
that transforms vultures into beautiful black
    race horses.

Yes, the horses are waiting at the starting gate.
Now the sound of the gun and this fantastic race begins.
The horses are circling the track.

The Pill Versus the Springhill Mine Disaster

When you take your pill
it's like a mine disaster.
I think of all the people
  lost inside of you.

After Halloween Slump

My magic is down.
My spells mope around
the house like sick old dogs
with bloodshot eyes
watering cold wet noses.

My charms are in a pile
in the corner like the
dirty shirts of a summer fatman.

One of my potions died
last night in the pot.
It looks like a cracked
Egyptian tablecloth.

Gee, You're so Beautiful That It's Starting to Rain

Oh, Marcia,
I want your long blonde beauty
to be taught in high school,
so kids will learn that God
lives like music in the skin
and sounds like a sunshine harpsicord.
I want high school report cards
  to look like this:

Playing with Gentle Glass Things
  A

Computer Magic
  A

Writing Letters to Those You Love
  A

Finding out about Fish
  A

Marcia's Long Blonde Beauty
  A+!

The Nature Poem

The moon
is Hamlet
on a motorcycle
coming down
a dark road.
He is wearing
a black leather
jacket and
boots.
I have
nowhere
to go.
I will ride
all night.

The Day They Busted the Grateful Dead

The day they busted the Grateful Dead
rain stormed against San Francisco
like hot swampy scissors cutting Justice
into the evil clothes that alligators wear.

The day they busted the Grateful Dead
was like a flight of winged alligators
carefully measuring marble with black
   rubber telescopes.

The day they busted the Grateful Dead
turned like the wet breath of alligators
blowing up balloons the size of the
   Hall of Justice.

The Harbor

Torn apart by the storms of love
and put back together by the calms
    of love,

I lie here in a harbor
that does not know
where your body ends
and my body begins.

Fish swim between our ribs
and sea gulls cry like mirrors
    to our blood.

The Garlic Meat Lady from

We're cooking dinner tonight.
I'm making a kind of Stonehenge
　　stroganoff.
Marcia is helping me.　You
already know the legend
　　of her beauty.
I've asked her to rub garlic
on the meat.　She takes
each piece of meat like a lover
and rubs it gently with garlic.
I've never seen anything like this
　　before.　Every orifice
of the meat is explored, caressed
　　relentlessly with garlic.
There is a passion here that would
drive a deaf saint to learn
the violin and play Beethoven at
　　Stonehenge.

In a Cafe

I watched a man in a cafe fold a slice of bread
as if he were folding a birth certificate or looking
at the photograph of a dead lover.

Boo, Forever

Spinning like a ghost
on the bottom of a
    top,
I'm haunted by all
the space that I
will live without
    you.

"In watermelon sugar the deeds were
done and done again as my life is
done in watermelon sugar."

Writing 21

RICHARD BRAUTIGAN

IN
WATERMELON
SUGAR

Book One:
In Watermelon Sugar

In Watermelon Sugar

IN WATERMELON SUGAR the deeds were done and done again as my life is done in watermelon sugar. I'll tell you about it because I am here and you are distant.

Wherever you are, we must do the best we can. It is so far to travel, and we have nothing here to travel, except watermelon sugar. I hope this works out.

I live in a shack near iDEATH. I can see iDEATH out the window. It is beautiful. I can also see it with my eyes closed and touch it. Right now it is cold and turns like something in the hand of a child. I do not know what that thing could be.

There is a delicate balance in iDEATH. It suits us.

The shack is small but pleasing and comfortable as my life and made from pine, watermelon sugar and stones as just about everything here is.

Our lives we have carefully constructed from watermelon sugar and then travelled to the length of our dreams, along roads lined with pines and stones.

I have a bed, a chair, a table and a large chest that I keep my things in. I have a lantern that burns watermelontrout oil at night.

That is something else. I'll tell you about it later. I have a gentle life.

I go to the window and look out again. The sun is shining at the long edge of a cloud. It is Tuesday and the sun is golden.

I can see piney woods and the rivers that flow from those piney woods. The rivers are cold and clear and there are trout in the rivers.

Some of the rivers are only a few inches wide.

I know a river that is half-an-inch wide. I know because I measured it and sat beside it for a whole day. It started raining in the middle of the afternoon. We call everything a river here. We're that kind of people.

I can see fields of watermelons and the rivers that flow through them. There are many bridges in the piney woods and in the fields of watermelons. There is a bridge in front of this shack.

Some of the bridges are made of wood, old and stained silver like rain, and some of the bridges are made of stone gathered from a great distance and built in the order of that distance, and some of the bridges are made of watermelon sugar. I like those bridges best.

We make a great many things out of watermelon sugar here —I'll tell you about it—including this book being written near iDEATH.

All this will be gone into, travelled in watermelon sugar.

2

Margaret

THIS MORNING there was a knock at the door. I could tell who it was by the way they knocked, and I heard them coming across the bridge.

They stepped on the only board that makes any noise. They always step on it. I have never been able to figure this out. I have thought a great deal about why they always step on that same board, how they cannot miss it, and now they stood outside my door, knocking.

I did not acknowledge their knocking because I just wasn't interested. I did not want to see them. I knew what they would be about and did not care for it.

Finally they stopped knocking and went back across the bridge and they, of course, stepped on the same board: a long board with the nails not lined up right, built years ago and no way to fix it, and then they were gone, and the board was silent.

I can walk across the bridge hundreds of times without stepping on that board, but Margaret always steps on it.

My Name

I GUESS YOU ARE KIND OF CURIOUS as to who I am, but I am one of those who do not have a regular name. My name depends on you. Just call me whatever is in your mind.

If you are thinking about something that happened a long time ago: Somebody asked you a question and you did not know the answer.

That is my name.

Perhaps it was raining very hard.

That is my name.

Or somebody wanted you to do something. You did it. Then they told you what you did was wrong—"Sorry for the mistake,"—and you had to do something else.

That is my name.

Perhaps it was a game that you played when you were a child or something that came idly into your mind when you were old and sitting in a chair near the window.

That is my name.

Or you walked someplace. There were flowers all around.

That is my name.

Perhaps you stared into a river. There was somebody near you who loved you. They were about to touch you. You could feel this before it happened. Then it happened.

4

That is my name.

Or you heard someone calling from a great distance. Their voice was almost an echo.

That is my name.

Perhaps you were lying in bed, almost ready to go to sleep and you laughed at something, a joke unto yourself, a good way to end the day.

That is my name.

Or you were eating something good and for a second forgot what you were eating, but still went on, knowing it was good.

That is my name.

Perhaps it was around midnight and the fire tolled like a bell inside the stove.

That is my name.

Or you felt bad when she said that thing to you. She could have told it to someone else: Somebody who was more familiar with her problems.

That is my name.

Perhaps the trout swam in the pool but the river was only eight inches wide and the moon shone on iDEATH and the watermelon fields glowed out of proportion, dark and the moon seemed to rise from every plant.

That is my name.

And I wish Margaret would leave me alone.

Fred

A LITTLE WHILE after Margaret left, Fred came by. He was not involved with the bridge. He only used it to get to my shack. He had nothing else to do with the bridge. He only walked across it to get to my place.

He just opened the door and came in. "Hi," he said. "What's up?"

"Nothing much," I said. "Just working away here."

"I just came from the Watermelon Works," Fred said. "I want you to go down there tomorrow morning with me. I want to show you something about the plank press."

"All right," I said.

"Good," he said. "I'll see you tonight at dinner down at iDEATH. I hear Pauline is going to cook dinner tonight. That means we'll have something good. I'm a little tired of Al's cooking. The vegetables are always overdone, and I'm tired of carrots, too. If I eat another carrot this week I'll scream."

"Yeah, Pauline's a good cook," I said. I wasn't really too much interested in food at the time. I wanted to get back to my work, but Fred is my buddy. We've had a lot of good times together.

Fred had something strange-looking sticking out of the pocket of his overalls. I was curious about it. It looked like something I had never seen before.

6

"What's that in your pocket, Fred?"

"I found it today coming through the woods up from the Watermelon Works. I don't know what it is myself. I've never seen anything like it before. What do you think it is?"

He took it out of his pocket and handed it to me. I didn't know how to hold it. I tried to hold it like you would hold a flower and a rock at the same time.

"How do you hold it?" I said.

"I don't know. I don't know anything about it."

"It looks like one of those things inBOIL and his gang used to dig up down at the Forgotten Works. I've never seen anything like it," I said, and gave it back to Fred.

"I'll show it to Charley," he said. "Maybe Charley will know. He knows about everything there is."

"Yeah, Charley knows a lot," I said.

"Well, I guess I had better be going," Fred said. He put the thing back in his overalls. "I'll see you at dinner," he said.

"OK."

Fred went out the door. He crossed the bridge without stepping on that board Margaret always steps on and couldn't miss if the bridge were seven miles wide.

Charley's Idea

AFTER FRED LEFT it felt good to get back to writing again, to dip my pen in watermelonseed ink and write upon these sheets of sweet-smelling wood made by Bill down at the shingle factory.

Here is a list of the things that I will tell you about in this book. There's no use saving it until later. I might as well tell you now where you're at—

1:   iDEATH. (A good place.)

2:   Charley (My friend.)

3:   The tigers and how they lived and how beautiful they were and how they died and how they talked to me while they ate my parents, and how I talked back to them and how they stopped eating my parents, though it did not help my parents any, nothing could help them by then, and we talked for a long time and one of the tigers helped me with my arithmetic, then they told me to go away while they finished eating my parents, and I went away. I returned later that night to burn the shack down. That's what we did in those days.

4:   The Statue of Mirrors.

5:   Old Chuck.

6:   The long walks I take at night. Sometimes I stand for hours at a single place, without hardly moving. (I've had the wind stop in my hand.)

8

7:     The Watermelon Works.
8:     Fred. (My buddy.)
9:     The baseball park.
10:    The aqueduct.
11:    Doc Edwards and the schoolteacher.
12:    The beautiful trout hatchery at iDEATH and how it was
built and the things that happen there. (It's a swell place for
dancing.)
13:    The Tomb Crew, the Shaft and the Shaft Gallows.
14:    A waitress.
15:    Al, Bill, others.
16:    The town.
17:    The sun and how it changes. (Very interesting.)
18:    inBOIL and that gang of his and the place where they
used to dig, the Forgotten Works, and all the terrible things they
did, and what happened to them, and how quiet and nice things
are around here now that they are dead.
19:    Conversations and things that happen here day to day.
(Work, baths, breakfast and dinner.)
20:    Margaret and that other girl who carried the lantern
at night and never came close.
21:    All of our statues and the places where we bury our
dead, so that they are forever with light coming out of their
tombs.
22:    My life lived in watermelon sugar. (There must be
worse lives.)
23:    Pauline. (She is my favorite. You'll see.)
24:    And this the twenty-fourth book written in 171 years.
Last month Charley said to me, "You don't seem to like making
statues or doing anything else. Why don't you write a book?

"The last one was written thirty-five years ago. It's about time
somebody wrote another book."

Then he scratched his head and said, "Gee, I remember it was
written thirty-five years ago, but I can't remember what it was
about. There used to be a copy of it in the sawmill."

"Do you know who wrote it?" I said.

"No," he said. "But he was like you. He didn't have a regular name."

I asked him what the other books were about, the twenty-three previous ones, and he said that he thought one of them was about owls.

"Yeah, it was about owls, and then there was a book about pine needles, very boring, and then there was one about the Forgotten Works, theories on how it got started and where it came from.

"The guy who wrote the book, his name was Mike, he took a long trip into the Forgotten Works. He went in maybe a hundred miles and was gone for weeks. He went beyond those high Piles we can see on clear days. He said that there were Piles beyond those that were even higher.

"He wrote a book about his journey into the Forgotten Works. It wasn't a bad book, a lot better than the books we find in the Forgotten Works. Those are terrible books.

"He said he was lost for days and came across things that were two miles long and green. He refused to furnish any other details about them, even in his book. Just said they were two miles long and green.

"That's his tomb down by that statue of a frog."

"I know that tomb well," I said. "He has blond hair and he's wearing a pair of rust-colored overalls."

"Yeah, that's him," Charley said.

Sundown

AFTER I FINISHED WRITING for the day it was close to sundown
and dinner would be ready soon down at iDEATH.

I looked forward to seeing Pauline and eating what she would
cook and seeing her at dinner and maybe I would see her after
dinner. We might go for a long walk, maybe along the aqueduct.

Then maybe we would go to her shack for the night or stay
at iDEATH or come back up here, if Margaret wouldn't knock the
door down the next time she came by.

The sun was going down over the Piles in the Forgotten
Works. They turned back far beyond memory and glowed in
the sundown.

The Gentle Cricket

I WENT OUT AND STOOD on the bridge for a while and looked down at the river below. It was three feet wide. There were a couple of statues standing in the water. One of them was my mother. She was a good woman. I made it five years ago.

The other statue was a cricket. I did not make that one. Somebody else made it a long time ago in the time of the tigers. It is a very gentle statue.

I like my bridge because it is made of all things: wood and the distant stones and gentle planks of watermelon sugar.

I walked down to iDEATH through a long cool twilight that passed like a tunnel over me. I lost sight of iDEATH when I passed into the piney woods and the trees smelled cold and they were growing steadily darker.

Lighting the Bridges

I LOOKED UP through the pines and saw the evening star. It glowed a welcoming red from the sky, for that is the color of our stars here. They are always that color.

I counted a second evening star on the opposite side of the sky, not as imposing but just as beautiful as the one that arrived first.

I came upon the real bridge and the abandoned bridge. They were side by side across a river. Trout were jumping in the river. A trout about twenty inches long jumped. I thought it was a rather nice fish. I knew I would remember it for a long time.

I saw somebody coming up the road. It was Old Chuck coming up from iDEATH to light the lanterns on the real bridge and the abandoned bridge. He was walking slowly because he is a very old man.

Some say that he is too old to light the bridges and that he should just stay down at iDEATH and take it easy. But Old Chuck likes to light the lanterns and come back in the morning and put them out.

Old Chuck says that everybody should have something to do and lighting those bridges is his thing to do. Charley agrees with him. "Let Old Chuck light the bridges if he feels like it. It keeps him out of mischief."

13

This is a kind of joke because Old Chuck must be ninety years old if he's a day and mischief has passed far beyond him, moving at the speed of decades.

Old Chuck has bad eyes and did not see me until he was almost on top of me. I waited for him. "Hello, Chuck," I said.

"Good evening," he said. "I've come to light the bridges. How are you this evening? I've come to light the bridges. Beautiful evening, isn't it?"

"Yes," I said. "Lovely."

Old Chuck went over to the abandoned bridge and took a six-inch match out of his overalls and lit the lantern on the iDEATH side of the bridge. The abandoned bridge has been that way since the time of the tigers.

In those days two tigers were trapped on the bridge and killed and then the bridge was set on fire. The fire only destroyed part of the bridge.

The bodies of the tigers fell into the river and you can still see their bones lying on the bottom in the sandy places and lodged in the rocks and scattered here and there: small bones and rib bones and part of a skull.

There is a statue in the river alongside the bones. It is the statue of somebody who was killed by the tigers a long time ago. Nobody knows who they were.

They never repaired the bridge and now it is the abandoned bridge. There is a lantern at each end of the bridge. Old Chuck lights them every evening, though some people say he is too old.

The real bridge is made entirely of pine. It is a covered bridge and always dark inside like an ear. The lanterns are in the shape of faces.

One face is that of a beautiful child and the other face is that of a trout. Old Chuck lit the lanterns with the long matches from his overalls.

The lanterns on the abandoned bridge are tigers.

"I'll walk with you down to iDEATH," I said.

"Oh no," Old Chuck said. "I'm too slow. You'll be late for

14

dinner."

"What about you?" I said.

"I've already eaten. Pauline gave me something to eat just before I left."

"What are we having for dinner?" I said.

"No," Old Chuck said, smiling. "Pauline told me if I met you on the road not to tell you what the dinner is tonight. She made me promise."

"That Pauline," I said.

"She made me promise," he said.

iDEATH

IT WAS ABOUT DARK when I arrived at iDEATH. The two evening stars were now shining side by side. The smaller one had moved over to the big one. They were very close now, almost touching, and then they went together and became one very large star.

I don't know if things like that are fair or not.

There were lights on down at iDEATH. I watched them as I came down the hill out of the woods. They looked warm, calling and cheery.

Just before I arrived at iDEATH, it changed. iDEATH's like that: always changing. It's for the best. I walked up the stairs to the front porch and opened the door and went in.

I walked across the living room toward the kitchen. There was nobody in the room, nobody sitting on the couches along the river. That's where people usually gather in the room or they stand in the trees by the big rocks, but there was nobody there either. There were many lanterns shining along the river and in the trees. It was very close to dinner.

When I got on the other side of the room, I could smell something good coming out of the kitchen. I left the room and walked down the hall that follows beneath the river. I could hear the river above me, flowing out of the living room. The river sounded fine.

16

The hall was as dry as anything and I could smell good things coming up the hall from the kitchen.

Almost everybody was in the kitchen: that is, those who take their meals at iDEATH. Charley and Fred were talking about something. Pauline was just getting ready to serve dinner. Everybody was sitting down. She was happy to see me. "Hi, stranger," she said.

"What's for dinner?" I said.

"Stew," she said. "The way you like it."

"Great," I said.

She gave me a nice smile and I sat down. Pauline was wearing a new dress and I could see the pleasant outlines of her body.

The dress had a low front and I could see the delicate curve of her breasts. I was quite pleased by everything. The dress smelled sweet because it was made from watermelon sugar.

"How's the book coming?" Charley said.

"Fine," I said. "Just fine."

"I hope it's not about pine needles," he said.

Pauline served me first. She gave me a great big helping of stew. Everybody was aware of me being served first and the size of the helping, and everybody smiled, for they knew what it meant, and they were happy for the thing that was going on.

Most of them did not like Margaret any more. Almost everybody thought that she had conspired with inBOIL and that gang of his, though there had never been any real evidence.

"This stew really tastes good," Fred said. He put a big spoonful of stew in his mouth, almost spilling some on his overalls. "Ummmm—good," he repeated and then said under his breath, "A lot better than carrots."

Al almost heard him. He looked hard for a second over at Fred, but he didn't quite catch it because he relaxed then and said, "It certainly is, Fred."

Pauline laughed slightly, for she had heard Fred's comment and I gave her a look as if to say: Don't laugh too hard, deary. You know how Al is about his cooking.

Pauline nodded understandingly.

"Just as long as it isn't about pine needles," Charley repeated, though a good ten minutes had passed since he'd said anything and that had been about pine needles, too.

The Tigers

AFTER DINNER Fred said that he would do the dishes. Pauline said oh no, but Fred insisted by actually starting to clear the table. He picked up some spoons and plates, and that settled it.

Charley said that he thought he would go in the living room and sit by the river and smoke a pipe. Al yawned. The other guys said that they would do other things, and went off to do them.

And then Old Chuck came in.

"What took you so long?" Pauline said.

"I decided to rest by the river. I fell asleep and had a long dream about the tigers. I dreamt they were back again."

"Sounds horrible," Pauline said. She shivered and kind of drew her shoulders in like a bird and put her hands on them.

"No, it was all right," Old Chuck said. He sat down in a chair. It took him a long time to sit down and then it was as if the chair had grown him, he was in so close.

"This time they were different," he said. "They played musical instruments and went for long walks in the moon.

"They stopped and played by the river. Their instruments looked nice. They sang, too. You remember how beautiful their voices were."

Pauline shivered again.

19

"Yes," I said. "They had beautiful voices but I never heard them singing."

"They were singing in my dream. I remember the music but I can't remember the words. They were good songs, too, and there was nothing frightening about them. Perhaps I am an old man," he said.

"No, they had beautiful voices," I said.

"I liked their songs," he said. "Then I woke up and it was cold. I could see the lanterns on the bridges. Their songs were like the lanterns, burning oil."

"I was a little worried about you," Pauline said.

"No," he said. "I sat down in the grass and leaned up against a tree and fell asleep and had a long dream about the tigers, and they sang songs but I can't remember the words. Their instruments were nice, too. They looked like the lanterns."

Old Chuck's voice slowed down. His body kept relaxing until it seemed as if he had always been in that chair, his arms gently resting on watermelon sugar.

More Conversation at iDEATH

PAULINE AND I went into the living room and sat down on a couch in the grove of trees by the big pile of rocks. There were lanterns all around us.

I took her hand in mine. Her hand had a lot of strength gained through the process of gentleness and that strength made my hand feel secure, but there was a certain excitement, too.

She sat very close to me. I could feel the warmth of her body through her dress. In my mind the warmth was the same color as her dress, a kind of golden.

"How's the book coming along?" she said.

"Fine," I said.

"What's it about?" she said.

"Oh, I don't know," I said.

"Is it a secret?" she said, smiling.

"No," I said.

"Is it a romance like some of the books from the Forgotten Works?"

"No," I said. "It's not like those books."

"I remember when I was a child," she said. "We used to burn those books for fuel. There were so many of them. They burned for a long time, but there aren't that many now."

"No, it's just a book," I said.

21

"All right," she said. "I'll get off you, but you can't blame a person for being curious. Nobody has written a book here for so long. Certainly not in my lifetime."

Fred came in from washing the dishes. He saw us up in the trees. Lanterns illuminated us.

"Hello, up there," he yelled.

"Hi," we shouted down.

Fred walked up to us, crossing a little river that flowed into the main river at iDEATH. He came across a small metal bridge that rang out his footsteps. I believe that bridge was found in the Forgotten Works by inBOIL. He brought it down here and put it in.

"Thanks for doing the dishes," Pauline said.

"My pleasure," Fred said. "I'm sorry to bother you people, but I just thought I would come up and remind you about meeting me down at the plank press tomorrow morning. There's something I want to show you down there."

"I haven't forgotten," I said. "What's it about?"

"I'll show you tomorrow."

"Good."

"That's all I wanted to say. I know you people have a lot to talk about, so I'll go now. That certainly was a good dinner, Pauline."

"Do you still have that thing you showed me today?" I said. "I'd like Pauline to see it."

"What thing?" Pauline said.

"Something Fred found in the woods today."

"No, I don't have it," Fred said. "I left it in my shack. I'll show it to you tomorrow at breakfast."

"What is it?" Pauline said.

"We don't know what it is," I said.

"Yeah, it's a strange-looking thing," Fred said. "It's like one of those things from the Forgotten Works."

"Oh," Pauline said.

"Well, anyway, I'll show it to you tomorrow at breakfast."

22

"Good," she said. "I look forward to seeing it. Whatever it is. Sounds pretty mysterious."

"OK, then," Fred said. "I'll be going now. Just wanted to remind you about seeing me tomorrow at the plank press. It's kind of important."

"Don't feel as if you should rush off," I said. "Join us for a while. Sit down."

"No, no, no. Thank you, anyway," Fred said. "There's something I have to do up at my shack."

"OK," I said.

"Good-bye."

"Thanks again for doing the dishes," Pauline said.

"Think nothing of it."

A Lot of Good Nights

IT WAS NOW GETTING LATE and Pauline and I went down to say good night to Charley. We could barely see him sitting down on his couch, near the statues that he likes and the place where he builds a small fire to warm himself on cold nights.

Bill had joined him and they were sitting there together, talking with great interest about something. Bill was waving his arms in the air to show a part of the conversation.

"We came down to say good night," I said, interrupting them.

"Oh, hi," Charley said. "Yeah, good night. I mean, how are you people doing?"

"OK," I said.

"That was a wonderful dinner," Bill said.

"Yeah, that was really fine," Charley said. "Good stew."

"Thank you."

"See you tomorrow," I said.

"Are you going to spend the night here at iDEATH?" Charley said.

"No," I said. "I'm going to spend the night with Pauline."

"That's good," Charley said.

"Good night."

"Good night."

"Good night."

"Good night."

Vegetables

PAULINE'S SHACK was about a mile from iDEATH. She doesn't spend much time there. It's beyond the town. There are about 375 of us here in watermelon sugar.

A lot of people live in the town, but some live in shacks at other places, and there are of course we who live at iDEATH.

There were just a few lights on in the town, other than the street lamps. Doc Edwards' light was on. He always has a lot of trouble sleeping at night. The schoolteacher's light was on, too. He was probably working on a lesson for the children.

We stopped on the bridge across the river. There were pale green lanterns on the bridge. They were in the shape of human shadows. Pauline and I kissed. Her mouth was moist and cool. Perhaps because of the night.

I heard a trout jump in the river, a late jumper. The trout made a narrow doorlike splash. There was a statue nearby. The statue was of a gigantic bean. That's right, a bean.

Somebody a long time ago liked vegetables and there are twenty or thirty statues of vegetables scattered here and there in watermelon sugar.

There is the statue of an artichoke near the shingle factory and a ten-foot carrot near the trout hatchery at iDEATH and a head of lettuce near the school and a bunch of onions near the entrance to the Forgotten Works and there are other vegetable statues near people's shacks and a rutabaga by the ball park.

A little ways from my shack there is the statue of a potato. I don't particularly care for it, but a long time ago somebody loved vegetables.

I once asked Charley if he knew who it was, but he said he didn't have the slightest idea. "Must have really liked vegetables, though," Charley'd said.

"Yeah," I'd said. "There's the statue of a potato right near my shack."

We continued up the road to Pauline's place. We passed by the Watermelon Works. It was silent and dark. Tomorrow morning it would be filled with light and activity. We could see the aqueduct. It was a long long shadow now.

We came to another bridge across a river. There were the usual lanterns on the bridge and statues in the river. There were a dozen or so pale lights coming up from the bottom of the river. They were tombs.

We stopped.

"The tombs look nice tonight," Pauline said.

"Certainly do," I said.

"There are mostly children here, aren't there?"

"Yes," I said.

"They're really beautiful tombs," Pauline said.

Moths fluttered above the light that came out of the river from the tombs below. There were five or six moths fluttering over each tomb.

Suddenly a big trout jumped out of the water above a tomb and got one of the moths. The other moths scattered and then came back again, and the same trout jumped again and got another moth. He was a smart old trout.

The trout did not jump any more and the moths fluttered peacefully above the light coming from the tombs.

Margaret Again

"How's MARGARET taking all this?" Pauline said.

"I don't know," I said.

"Is she hurt or mad or what? Do you know how she feels?" Pauline said. "Has she talked to you about it since you told her? She hasn't talked to me at all. I saw her yesterday near the Watermelon Works. I said hello but she walked past me without saying anything. She seemed terribly upset."

"I don't know how she feels," I said.

"I thought she'd be at iDEATH tonight, but she wasn't there," Pauline said. "I don't know why I thought she'd be there. I just had a feeling but I was wrong. Have you seen her?"

"No," I said.

"I wonder where she's staying," Pauline said.

"I think she's staying with her brother."

"I feel bad about this. Margaret and I were such good friends. All the years we've spent together at iDEATH," Pauline said. "We were almost like sisters. I'm sorry that things had to work out this way, but there was nothing we could do about it."

"The heart is something else. Nobody knows what's going to happen," I said.

"You're right," Pauline said.

She stopped and kissed me. Then we crossed over the bridge to her shack.

Pauline's Shack

PAULINE'S SHACK is made entirely of watermelon sugar, except the door that is a good-looking grayish-stained pine with a stone doorknob.

Even the windows are made of watermelon sugar. A lot of windows here are made of sugar. It's very hard to tell the difference between sugar and glass, the way sugar is used by Carl the windowmaker. It's just a thing that depends on who is doing it. It's a delicate art and Carl has it.

Pauline lit a lantern. It smelled fragrant burning with watermelontrout oil. We have a way here also of mixing watermelon and trout to make a lovely oil for our lanterns. We use it for all our lighting purposes. It has a gentle fragrance to it, and makes a good light.

Pauline's shack is very simple as all our shacks are simple. Everything was in its proper place. Pauline uses the shack just to get away from iDEATH for a few hours or a night if she feels like it.

All of us who stay at iDEATH have shacks to visit whenever we feel like it. I spend more time at my shack than anybody else. I usually just sleep one night a week at iDEATH. I of course take most of my meals there. We who do not have regular names spend a lot of time by ourselves. It suits us.

"Well, here we are," Pauline said. She looked beautiful in the light of the lantern. Her eyes sparkled.

"Please come here," I said. She came over to me and I kissed her mouth and then I touched her breasts. They felt so smooth and firm. I put my hand down the front of her dress.

"That feels good," she said.

"Let's try some more," I said.

"That would be good," she said.

We went over and lay upon her bed. I took her dress off. She had nothing on underneath. We did that for a while. Then I got up and took off my overalls and lay back down beside her.

A Love, a Wind

WE MADE a long and slow love. A wind came up and the windows trembled slightly, the sugar set fragilely ajar by the wind.

I liked Pauline's body and she said that she liked mine, too, and we couldn't think of anything to say.

The wind suddenly stopped and Pauline said, "What's that?"

"It's the wind."

The Tigers Again

AFTER MAKING LOVE we talked about the tigers. It was Pauline who started it. She was lying warmly beside me, and she wanted to talk about the tigers. She said that Old Chuck's dream got her thinking about them.

"I wonder why they could speak our language," she said.

"No one knows," I said. "But they could speak it. Charley says maybe we were tigers a long time ago and changed but they didn't. I don't know. It's an interesting idea, though."

"I never heard their voices," Pauline said. "I was just a child and there were only a few tigers left, old ones, and they barely came out of the hills. They were too old to be dangerous, and they were hunted all the time.

"I was six years old when they killed the last one. I remember the hunters bringing it to iDEATH. There were hundreds of people with them. The hunters said they had killed it up in the hills that day, and it was the last tiger.

"They brought the tiger to iDEATH and everybody came with them. They covered it with wood and soaked the wood down with watermelontrout oil. Gallons and gallons of it. I remember people threw flowers on the pile and stood around crying because it was the last tiger.

"Charley took a match and lit the fire. It burned with a great orange glow for hours and hours, and black smoke poured up into the air.

"It burned until there was nothing left but ashes, and then the men began right then and there building the trout hatchery at iDEATH, right over the spot where the tiger had been burned. It's hard to think of that now when you're down there dancing.

"I guess you remember all this," Pauline said. "You were there, too. You were standing beside Charley."

"That's right," I said. "They had beautiful voices."

"I never heard them" she said.

"Perhaps that was for the best," I said.

"Maybe you're right," she said. "Tigers," and was soon fast asleep in my arms. Her sleep tried to become my arm, and then my body, but I wouldn't let it because I was suddenly very restless.

I got up and put on my overalls and went for one of the long walks I take at night.

Arithmetic

THE NIGHT WAS COOL and the stars were red. I walked down by the Watermelon Works. That's where we process the watermelons into sugar. We take the juice from the watermelons and cook it down until there's nothing left but sugar, and then we work it into the shape of this thing that we have: our lives.

I sat down on a couch by the river. Pauline had gotten me thinking about the tigers. I sat there and thought about them, how they killed and ate my parents.

We lived together in a shack by the river. My father raised watermelons and my mother baked bread. I was going to school. I was nine years old and having trouble with arithmetic.

One morning the tigers came in while we were eating breakfast and before my father could grab a weapon they killed him and they killed my mother. My parents didn't even have time to say anything before they were dead. I was still holding the spoon from the mush I was eating.

"Don't be afraid," one of the tigers said. "We're not going to hurt you. We don't hurt children. Just sit there where you are and we'll tell you a story."

One of the tigers started eating my mother. He bit her arm off and started chewing on it. "What kind of story would you like to hear? I know a good story about a rabbit."

"I don't want to hear a story," I said.

"OK," the tiger said, and he took a bite out of my father. I sat there for a long time with the spoon in my hand, and then I put it down.

"Those were my folks," I said, finally.

"We're sorry," one of the tigers said. "We really are."

"Yeah," the other tiger said. "We wouldn't do this if we didn't have to, if we weren't absolutely forced to. But this is the only way we can keep alive."

"We're just like you," the other tiger said. "We speak the same language you do. We think the same thoughts, but we're tigers."

"You could help me with my arithmetic," I said.

"What's that?" one of the tigers said.

"My arithmetic."

"Oh, your arithmetic."

"Yeah."

"What do you want to know?" one of the tigers said.

"What's nine times nine?"

"Eighty-one," a tiger said.

"What's eight times eight?"

"Fifty-six," a tiger said.

I asked them half a dozen other questions: six times six, seven times four, etc. I was having a lot of trouble with arithmetic. Finally the tigers got bored with my questions and told me to go away.

"OK," I said. "I'll go outside."

"Don't go too far," one of the tigers said. "We don't want anyone to come up here and kill us."

"OK."

They both went back to eating my parents. I went outside and sat down by the river. "I'm an orphan," I said.

I could see a trout in the river. He swam directly at me and then he stopped right where the river ends and the land begins. He stared at me.

34

"What do you know about anything?" I said to the trout.

That was before I went to live at IDEATH.

After about an hour or so the tigers came outside and stretched and yawned.

"It's a nice day," one of the tigers said.

"Yeah," the other tiger said. "Beautiful."

"We're awfully sorry we had to kill your parents and eat them. Please try to understand. We tigers are not evil. This is just a thing we have to do."

"All right," I said. "And thanks for helping me with my arithmetic."

"Think nothing of it."

The tigers left.

I went over to IDEATH and told Charley that the tigers had eaten my parents.

"What a shame," he said.

"The tigers are so nice. Why do they have to go and do things like that?" I said.

"They can't help themselves," Charley said. "I like the tigers, too. I've had a lot of good conversations with them. They're very nice and have a good way of stating things, but we're going to have to get rid of them. Soon."

"One of them helped me with my arithmetic."

"They're very helpful," Charley said. "But they're dangerous. What are you going to do now?"

"I don't know," I said.

"How would you like to stay here at IDEATH?" Charley said.

"That sounds good," I said.

"Fine. Then it's settled," Charley said.

That night I went back to the shack and set fire to it. I didn't take anything with me and went to live at IDEATH. That was twenty years ago, though it seems like it was only yesterday: What's eight times eight?

35

She Was

FINALLY I STOPPED THINKING about the tigers and started back to
Pauline's shack. I would think about the tigers another day.
There would be many.

I wanted to stay the night with Pauline. I knew that she would
be beautiful in her sleep, waiting for me to return. She was.

A Lamb at False Dawn

PAULINE BEGAN TALKING in her sleep at false dawn from under the watermelon covers. She told a little story about a lamb going for a walk.

"The lamb sat down in the flowers," she said. "The lamb was all right," and that was the end of the story.

Pauline often talks in her sleep. Last week she sang a little song. I forget how it went.

I put my hand on her breast. She stirred in her sleep. I took my hand off her breast and she was quiet again.

She felt very good in bed. There was a nice sleepy smell coming from her body. Perhaps that is where the lamb sat down.

The Watermelon Sun

I WOKE UP before Pauline and put on my overalls. A crack of gray sun shone through the window and lay quietly on the floor. I went over and put my foot in it, and then my foot was gray.

I looked out the window and across the fields and piney woods and the town to the Forgotten Works. Everything was touched with gray: Cattle grazing in the fields and the roofs of the shacks and the big Piles in the Forgotten Works all looked like dust. The very air itself was gray.

We have an interesting thing with the sun here. It shines a different color every day. No one knows why this is, not even Charley. We grow the watermelons in different colors the best we can.

This is how we do it: Seeds gathered from a gray watermelon picked on a gray day and then planted on a gray day will make more gray watermelons.

It is really very simple. The colors of the days and the watermelons go like this—

Monday: red watermelons.
Tuesday: golden watermelons.
Wednesday: gray watermelons.
Thursday: black, soundless watermelons.
Friday: white watermelons.

Saturday: blue watermelons.

Sunday: brown watermelons.

Today would be a day of gray watermelons. I like best tomorrow: the black, soundless watermelon days. When you cut them they make no noise, and taste very sweet.

They are very good for making things that have no sound. I remember there was a man who used to make clocks from the black, soundless watermelons and his clocks were silent.

The man made six or seven of these clocks and then he died.

There is one of the clocks hanging over his grave. It is hanging from the branches of an apple tree and sways in the winds that go up and down the river. It of course does not keep time any more.

Pauline woke up while I was putting my shoes on.

"Hello," she said, rubbing her eyes. "You're up. I wonder what time it is."

"It's about six."

"I have to cook breakfast this morning at iDEATH," she said. "Come over here and give me a kiss and then tell me what you would like for breakfast."

Hands

WE WALKED BACK TO IDEATH, holding hands. Hands are very nice things, especially after they have travelled back from making love.

Margaret Again, Again

I SAT IN THE KITCHEN at iDEATH, watching Pauline make the batter for hot cakes, my favorite food. She put a lot of flour and eggs and good things into a great blue bowl and stirred the batter with a big wooden spoon, almost too large for her hand.

She was wearing a real nice dress and her hair was combed on top of her head and I had stopped and picked some flowers for her hair when we walked down the road.

They were bluebells.

"I wonder if Margaret will be here today," she said. "I'll be glad when we're talking again."

"Don't worry about it," I said. "Everything will be all right."

"It's just—well, Margaret and I have been such good friends. I'd always liked you before, but I never thought we'd ever be anything but friends.

"You and Margaret were so close for years. I just hope everything works out, and Margaret finds someone new and will be my friend again."

"Don't worry."

Fred came into the kitchen just to say, "Ummmm—hot cakes," and then left.

Strawberries

CHARLEY MUST HAVE EATEN a dozen hot cakes himself. I have never seen him eat so many hot cakes, and Fred ate a few more than Charley.

It was quite a sight.

There was also a big platter of bacon and lots of fresh milk and a big pot of strong coffee, and there was a bowl of fresh strawberries, too.

A girl came by from the town and left them off just before breakfast. She was a gentle girl.

Pauline said, "Thank you, and what a lovely dress you have on this morning. Did you make it yourself? You must have because it's so pretty."

"Oh, thank you," the girl said, blushing. "I just wanted to bring some strawberries to iDEATH for breakfast, so I got up very early and gathered them down by the river."

Pauline ate one of the berries and gave one of them to me. "They are such fine berries," Pauline said. "You must know a good place to get them, and you must show me where that place is."

"It's right near that statue of a rutabaga by the ball park, just down from where that funny green bridge is," the girl said. She was about fourteen years old and very pleased that her

42

strawberries were a big hit at iDEATH.

All of the strawberries were eaten at breakfast, and again as for the hot cakes: "These are really wonderful hot cakes," Charley said.

"Would you like some more?" Pauline said.

"Maybe another one if there is any more batter."

"There's plenty," Pauline said. "How about you, Fred?"

"Well, maybe just one more."

The Schoolteacher

AFTER BREAKFAST I kissed Pauline while she was washing the dishes and went with Fred down to the Watermelon Works to see something he wanted to show me about the plank press.

We took a long leisurely stroll down there, through the morning of a gray sun. It looked like it might rain but of course it would not. The first rain of the year would not start until the 12th day of October.

"Margaret wasn't there this morning," Fred said.

"No, she wasn't," I said.

We stopped and talked to the schoolteacher who was taking his students for a walk in the woods. While we talked to him all the children sat down in the grass nearby, and were kind of gathered together like a ring of mushrooms or daisies.

"Well, how's the book coming?" the schoolteacher said.

"All right," I said.

"I'll be very curious to see it," the schoolteacher said. "You always had a way with words. I still remember that essay you wrote on weather when you were in the sixth grade. That was quite something.

"Your description of the winter clouds was very accurate and quite moving at the same time and contained a certain amount of poetic content. Yes, I am quite interested in reading your book. Will you give any hints on what it is about?"

Fred meanwhile looked very bored. He went and sat down with the children. He started talking to a boy about something.

"Have you expanded your essay on weather or is the book about something else?"

The boy was very interested in what Fred was saying. A couple of other kids moved closer.

"Oh, it's just coming along," I said. "It's pretty hard to talk about. But you'll be one of the first I'll show it to when it's done."

"I've always had faith in you as a writer," the schoolteacher said. "For a long time I thought about writing a book myself, but teaching absorbs just too much of my time."

Fred took something out of his pocket. He showed it to the boy. He looked at it and passed it on to the other children.

"Yes, I thought that I would write a book about teaching, but so far I've been too busy teaching to write. But it is very inspiring to me to have one of my former star pupils carry the glorious banner for what I myself have been too busy to do. Good luck."

"Thank you."

Fred put the thing back in his pocket and the schoolteacher got all of his students back on their feet, and off they went to the woods.

He was talking to them about something very important. I could tell because he pointed back at me, and then he pointed at a cloud that was drifting low overhead.

Under the Plank Press

As WE NEARED the Watermelon Works the air was full of the sweet smell of the sugar being boiled in the vats. There were great layers and strips and shapes of sugar hardening out in the sun: red sugar, golden sugar, gray sugar, black, soundless sugar, white sugar, blue sugar, brown sugar.

"The sugar sure looks good," Fred said.

"Yeah."

I waved at Ed and Mike, whose job it is to keep the birds off the sugar. They waved back, and then one of them began chasing after a bird.

There are about a dozen people who work at the Watermelon Works, and we went inside. There were great fires going under the two vats, and Peter was feeding wood into them. He looked hot and sweaty, but that was his natural condition.

"How's the sugar coming?" I said.

"Fine," he said. "Lot of sugar. How are things at iDEATH?"

"Good," I said.

"What's this about you and Pauline?"

"Just gossip," I said.

I like Pete. We've been friends for years. When I was a child I used to come down to the Watermelon Works and help him feed the fires.

46

"I'll bet Margaret's mad," he said. "I hear she's really pining for you. That's what her brother says. She's just pining away."

"I don't know about that," I said.

"What are you down here for?" he said.

"I just came down here to chuck a piece of wood in the fire," I said. I reached over and picked up a large pine knot and put it in the fire under a vat.

"Just like old times," he said.

The foreman came out of his office and joined us. He looked kind of tired.

"Hi, Edgar," I said.

"Hello," he said. "How are you? Good morning, Fred."

"Good morning, boss."

"What brings you down here?" Edgar said.

"Fred wants to show me something."

"What's that, Fred?" Edgar said.

"It's a private thing, boss."

"Oh. Well, show away, then."

"Will do, boss."

"It's always good to see you down here," Edgar said to me.

"You look kind of tired," I said.

"Yeah, I stayed up late last night."

"Well, get some sleep tonight," I said.

"That's what I'm planning on. As soon as I get off work I'm going straight home to bed. Don't even think I'll eat any dinner, just grab a snack."

"Sleep's good for you," Fred said.

"I guess I'd better get back to the office," Edgar said. "I've got some paper work to do. See you later."

"Yeah, good-bye, Edgar."

The foreman went back to his office, and I went with Fred to the plank press. That's where we make watermelon planks. Today they were making golden planks.

Fred is the straw boss and the rest of his crew was already there, turning out planks.

47

"Good morning," the crew said.

"Good morning," Fred said. "Let's stop this thing here for a minute."

One of the crew turned off the switch and Fred had me come over very close and get down on my hands and knees and crawl under the press until we came to a very dark place and then he lit a match and showed me a bat hanging upside down from a housing.

"What do you think of that?" Fred said.

"Yeah," I said, staring at the bat.

"I found him there a couple of days ago. Doesn't that beat everything?" he said.

"It's got a head start," I said.

Until Lunch

AFTER HAVING ADMIRED Fred's bat and crawled out from underneath the plank press, I told him that I had to go up to my shack and do some work: plant some flowers and things.

"Are you going to have lunch at iDEATH?" he said.

"No, I think I'll just have a snack downtown at the cafe later on. Why don't you join me, Fred?"

"OK," he said. "I think they're serving frankfurters and sauerkraut today."

"That was yesterday," one of his crew volunteered.

"You're right," Fred said. "Today's meat loaf. How does that sound?"

"All right," I said. "I'll see you for lunch, then. About twelve."

I left Fred supervising the plank press with big golden planks of watermelon sugar coming down the chain. The Watermelon Works was bubbling and drying away, sweet and gentle in the warm gray sun.

And Ed and Mike were chasing after birds. Mike was running a robin off.

The Tombs

On my way to the shack, I decided to go down to the river where they were putting in a new tomb and look at the trout that always gather out of a great curiosity when the tombs are put in.

I passed through the town. It was kind of quiet with just a few people on the streets. I saw Doc Edwards going somewhere carrying his bag, and I waved at him.

He waved back and made a motion to show that he was on a very important errand. Somebody was probably sick in the town. I waved him on.

There were a couple of old people sitting in rocking chairs on the front porch of the hotel. One of them was rocking and the other one was asleep. The one that was asleep had a newspaper in his lap.

I could smell bread baking in the bakery and there were two horses tied up in front of the general store. I recognized one of the horses as being from iDEATH.

I walked out of the town and passed by some trees that were at the edge of a little watermelon patch. The trees had moss hanging from them.

A squirrel ran up into the branches of a tree. His tail was missing. I wondered what had happened to his tail. I guess he lost it someplace.

I sat down on a couch by the river. There was a statue of grass beside the couch. The blades were made from copper and had been turned to their natural color by the rain weight of years.

There were four or five guys putting in the tomb. They were the Tomb Crew. The tomb was being put into the bottom of the river. That's how we bury our dead here. Of course we used a lot less tombs when the tigers were in bloom.

But now we bury them all in glass coffins at the bottoms of rivers and put foxfire in the tombs, so they glow at night and we can appreciate what comes next.

I saw a bunch of trout gathered together to watch the tomb being put in. They were nice-looking rainbow trout. There were perhaps a hundred of them in a very small space in the river. The trout have a great curiosity about this activity, and many of them gather to watch.

The Tomb Crew had sunk the Shaft into the river and the pump was going away. They were doing the glass inlay work now. Soon the tomb would be complete and the door would be opened when it was needed and someone would go inside to stay there for the ages.

The Grand Old Trout

I SAW A TROUT that I have known for a long time watching the tomb being put in. It was The Grand Old Trout, raised as a fingerling in the trout hatchery at iDEATH. I knew this because he had the little iDEATH bell fastened to his jaw. He is many years old and weighs many pounds and moves slowly with wisdom.

The Grand Old Trout usually spends all of its time upstream by the Statue of Mirrors. I had spent many hours in the past watching this trout in the deep pool there. I guess he had been curious about this particular tomb and had come down to watch it being put in.

I wondered about this because The Grand Old Trout usually shows very little interest in watching the tombs being put in. I guess because he has seen so many before.

I remember once they were putting in a tomb just a little ways down from the Statue of Mirrors and he didn't move an inch in all the days that it took because it was such a hard tomb to put in.

The tomb collapsed just before completion. Charley came down and shook his head sadly, and the tomb had to be done all over again.

But now the trout was watching very intently this tomb being put in. He was hovering just a few inches above the bottom and ten feet away from the Shaft.

I went down and crouched by the river. The trout were not scared at all by the closeness of my appearance. The Grand Old Trout looked over at me.

I believe he recognized me, for he stared at me for a couple of minutes, and then he turned back to watching the tomb being put in, the final inlay work being done.

I stayed there for a little while by the river and when I left to go to my shack, The Grand Old Trout turned and stared at me. He was still staring at me when I was gone from sight, I thought.

Book Two:
inBOIL

Nine Things

IT WAS GOOD to be back at my shack, but there was a note on the door from Margaret. I read the note and it did not please me and I threw it away, so not even time could find it.

I sat down at my table and looked out the window, down to iDEATH. I had a few things to do with pen and ink and did them rapidly and without mistake, and put them away written in watermelonseed ink upon these sheets of sweet smelling wood made by Bill down at the shingle factory.

Then I thought that I would plant some flowers out by the potato statue, a bunch of them in a circle around that seven-foot potato would look nice.

I went and got some seeds from the chest that I keep my things in and noticed that everything was ajar, and so before planting the seeds, I put everything back in order.

I have nine things, more or less: a child's ball (I can't remember which child), a present given me nine years ago by Fred, my essay on weather, some numbers (1-24), an extra pair of overalls, a piece of blue metal, something from the Forgotten Works, a lock of hair that needs washing.

I kept the seeds out because I was going to put them in the ground around the potato. I have a few other things that I keep in my room at iDEATH. I have a nice room there off toward the trout hatchery.

I went outside and planted the seeds around the potato and wondered again who liked vegetables so much, and where were they buried, under what river or had a tiger eaten them a long time ago when the tiger's beautiful voice had said, "I like your statues very much, especially that rutabaga by the ball park, but alas. . ."

Margaret Again, Again, Again

I SPENT A HALF AN HOUR or so pacing back and forth on the bridge, but I did not once find that board that Margaret always steps on, that board she could not miss if all the bridges in the world were put together, formed into one single bridge, she'd step on that board.

A Nap

SUDDENLY I FELT very tired and decided to take a nap before lunch and went into the shack and lay down in my bed. I looked up at the ceiling, at the beams of watermelon sugar. I stared at the grain and was soon fast asleep.

I had a couple of small dreams. One of them was about a moth. The moth was balanced on an apple.

Then I had a long dream, which was again the history of inBOIL and that gang of his and the terrible things that happened just a few short months ago.

Whiskey

InBOIL and that gang of his lived in a little bunch of lousy shacks with leaky roofs near the Forgotten Works. They lived there until they were dead. I think there were about twenty of them. All men, like inBOIL, that were no good.

First there was just inBOIL who lived there. He got in a big fight one night with Charley and told him to go to hell and said he would sooner live by the Forgotten Works than in iDEATH.

"To hell with iDEATH," he said, and went and built himself a lousy shack by the Forgotten Works. He spent his time digging around in there and making whiskey from things.

Then a couple of other men went and joined up with him and from time to time, every once in a while, a new man would join them. You could always tell who they would be.

Before they joined inBOIL's gang, they would always be unhappy and nervous and shifty or have "light fingers" and talk a lot about things that good people did not understand nor wanted to.

They would grow more and more nervous and no account and then finally you would hear about them having joined inBOIL's gang and now they were working with him in the Forgotten Works, and being paid in whiskey that inBOIL made from forgotten things.

Whiskey Again

INBOIL was about fifty years old, I guess, and was born and raised at iDEATH. I remember sitting upon his knee as a child and having him tell me stories. He knew some pretty good ones, too . . . and Margaret was there.

Then he turned bad. It happened over a couple of years. He kept getting mad at things that were of no importance and going off by himself to the trout hatchery at iDEATH.

He began spending a lot of time at the Forgotten Works, and Charley would ask him what he was doing and inBOIL would say, "Oh, nothing. Just off by myself."

"What kind of things do you find when you're digging down there?"

"Oh, nothing," inBOIL lied.

He became very removed from people and then his speech would be strange, slurred and his movements became jerky and his temper bad, and he spent a lot of time at night in the trout hatchery and sometimes he would laugh out loud and you could hear this enormous laugh that had now become his, echoing through the rooms and halls, and into the very changing of iDEATH: the indescribable way it changes that we like so much, that suits us.

The Big Fight

THE BIG FIGHT between inBOIL and Charley occurred at dinner one night. Fred was passing some mashed potatoes to me when it happened.

The fight had been building up for weeks. inBOIL's laughter had grown louder and louder until it was almost impossible to sleep at night.

inBOIL was drunk all the time, and he would listen to no one about anything, not even Charley. He wouldn't even listen to Charley. He told Charley to mind his own business. "Mind your own business."

One afternoon Pauline, who was just a child, found him passed out in the bathtub, singing dirty songs. She was frightened and he had a bottle of that stuff he brewed down at the Forgotten Works. He smelled horrible and it took three men to lift him out of the bathtub and get him to bed.

"Here are the mashed potatoes," Fred said.

I was just putting a big scoop of them on my plate to soak up the rest of the gravy when inBOIL, who had not touched a single bite of his fried chicken and it was growing cold in front of him, turned to Charley and said, "Do you know what's wrong with this place?"

"No, what's wrong, inBOIL? You seem to have all the answers these days. Tell me."

"I *will* tell you. This place stinks. This isn't iDEATH at all. This is just a figment of your imagination. All of you guys here are just a bunch of clucks, doing clucky things at your clucky iDEATH.

"iDEATH—ha, don't make me laugh. This place is nothing but a claptrap. You wouldn't know iDEATH if it walked up and bit you.

"I know more about iDEATH than all of you guys, especially Charley here who thinks he's something extra. I know more about iDEATH in my little finger than all you guys know put together.

"You haven't the slightest idea what's going on here. I know. I know. I know. To hell with your iDEATH. I've forgotten more iDEATH than you guys will ever know. I'm going down to the Forgotten Works to live. You guys can have this damn rat hole."

inBOIL got up and threw his fried chicken on the floor and stomped out of the place, travelling very unevenly. There was stunned silence at the table and no one could say anything for a long time.

Then Fred said, "Don't feel bad about it, Charley. He'll be sober tomorrow and everything will be different. He's just drunk again and as soon as he sobers up, he'll be better."

"No, I think he's gone for good," Charley said. "I hope it all works out for the best."

Charley looked very sad and we were all sad, too, because inBOIL was Charley's brother. We all sat there looking at our food.

Time

THE YEARS PASSED with inBOIL living down by the Forgotten
Works and gathering slowly a gang of men who were just
like him, believed in the things he did, and acted his way and
went digging in the Forgotten Works and drank whiskey brewed
from the things they found.

Sometimes they would sober up one of the gang and send
him into town to sell forgotten things that were particularly
beautiful or curious or books which we used for fuel then
because there were millions of them lying around in the Forgot-
ten Works.

They would get bread and food and whatnot for the forgotten
things and so lived without having to do anything besides dig
and drink.

Margaret grew up to be a very pretty young woman and we
went steady together. Margaret came over to my shack one day.

I could tell it was her even before she was there because I
heard her step on that board she always steps on, and it pleased
me and made my stomach tingle like a bell set ajar.

She knocked on the door.

"Come in, Margaret," I said.

She came in and kissed me. "What are you doing today?"
she said.

"I have to go down to iDEATH and work on my statue."

"Are you still working on that bell?" she said.

"Yes," I said. "It's coming along rather slowly. It's taking too long. I'll be glad when it's done. I'm tired of the thing."

"What are you going to do afterwards?" she said.

"I don't know. Is there anything you want to do, honey?"

"Yes," she said. "I want to go down to the Forgotten Works and poke around."

"Again?" I said. "You certainly like to spend a lot of time down there."

"It's a curious place," she said.

"You're about the only woman who likes that place. inBOIL and that gang of his put the other women off."

"I like it down there. inBOIL is harmless. All he wants to do is stay drunk."

"All right," I said. "It's nothing, honey. Meet me down at iDEATH later on. I'll be with you as soon as I put in a few more hours on that bell."

"Are you going down now?" she said.

"No, I have a few things I want to do here first."

"Can I help?" she said.

"No, they're just a few things I have to do alone."

"OK, then. I'll see you."

"Give me a kiss first," I said.

She came over and I held her in my arms very close and kissed Margaret upon the mouth, and then she went off laughing.

The Bell

AFTER WHILE I went down to iDEATH and worked on that bell. It was not coming at all and finally I was just sitting there on a chair, staring at it.

My chisel was hanging limply in my hand, and then I put it down on the table and absentmindedly covered it up with a rag.

Fred came in and saw me sitting there staring at the bell. He left without saying anything. It hardly even looked like a bell.

Finally Margaret came and rescued me. She was wearing a blue dress and had a ribbon in her hair and carried a basket to put things in that she found at the Forgotten Works.

"How's it coming?" she said.

"It's finished," I said.

"It doesn't look finished," she said.

"It's finished," I said.

Pauline

WE SAW Charley as we were leaving iDEATH. He was sitting on his favorite couch by the river, feeding little pieces of bread to some trout that had gathered there.

"Where you kids going?" he said.

"Oh, just out for a walk," Margaret said, before I could say anything.

"Well, have a good walk," he said. "Lovely day, isn't it? Great big beautiful blue sun shining away."

"It sure is," I said.

Pauline came into the room and walked over and joined us. "Hello, there," she said.

"Hi."

"What do you want for dinner, Charley?" she said.

"Roast beef," Charley said, joking.

"Well, that's what you'll have then."

"What a nice surprise," Charley said. "Is it my birthday?"

"No. How are you people?"

"We're fine," I said.

"We're going for a walk," Margaret said.

"That sounds like fun. See you later."

The Forgotten Works

NOBODY KNOWS how old the Forgotten Works are, reaching as they do into distances that we cannot travel nor want to.

Nobody has been very far into the Forgotten Works, except that guy Charley said who wrote a book about them, and I wonder what his trouble was, to spend weeks in there.

The Forgotten Works just go on and on and on and on and on and on and on and on and on. You get the picture. It's a big place, much bigger than we are.

Margaret and I went down there, holding hands for we were going steady, through the sun of a blue day and white luminous clouds drifting overhead.

We crossed over many rivers and walked by many things, and then we could see the sun reflecting off the roofs at inBOIL's bunch of leaky shacks which were at the entrance to the Forgotten Works.

There is a gate right there. Beside the gate is the statue of a forgotten thing. There is a sign above the gate that says:

THIS IS THE ENTRANCE TO THE FORGOTTEN WORKS
BE CAREFUL
YOU MIGHT GET LOST

A Conversation with Trash

INBOIL came out to greet us. His clothes were all wrinkled and dirty and so was he. He looked like a mess and he was drunk.

"Hello," he said. "Down here again, huh?" he said, more to Margaret than to me, though he looked at me when he said it. That's the kind of person INBOIL is.

"Just visiting," I said.

He laughed at that. A couple of other guys came out of shacks and stared at us. They all looked like INBOIL. They had made the same mess out of themselves by being evil and drinking that whiskey made from forgotten things.

One of them, a yellow-haired one, sat down on a pile of disgusting objects and just stared at us like he was an animal.

"Good afternoon, INBOIL, ' Margaret said.

"Same to you, pretty."

Some of INBOIL's trash laughed at that and I looked at them hard and they shut up. One of them wiped his hand across his mouth and went inside his shack.

"Just being social," INBOIL said. "Don't take no offense."

"We're just down here to look at the Forgotten Works," I said.

"Well, she's all yours," INBOIL said, pointing at the Forgotten Works that gradually towered above us until the big piles of forgotten things were mountains that went on for at least a million miles.

In There

YOU MIGHT GET LOST

and we walked through the gate into the Forgotten Works.
Margaret started poking around for things that she might like.

There were no plants growing and no animals living in the
Forgotten Works. There was not even so much as a blade of
grass in there, and the birds refused to fly over the place.

I sat down on something that looked like a wheel and watched
Margaret take a forgotten sticklike thing and poke around a
small pile of stuffed things.

I saw something lying at my feet. It was a piece of ice frozen
into the shape of a thumb, but the thumb had a hump on it.

It was a hunchback thumb and very cold but started to melt
in my hand.

The fingernail melted away and then I dropped the thing and
it lay at my feet, not melting any more, though the air was not
cold and the sun was hot and blue in the sky.

"Have you found anything you like?" I said.

The Master of the Forgotten Works

INBOIL came in and joined us. It did not overly please me to see him. He had a bottle of whiskey with him. His nose was red.

"Find anything you like?" INBOIL said.

"Not yet," Margaret said.

I gave INBOIL a dirty look but it rolled off him like water off a duck's back.

"I found some real good interesting things today," INBOIL said. "Just before I went to have lunch."

Lunch!

"They're about a quarter-of-a-mile in. I can show you the place," INBOIL said.

Before I could say no, Margaret said yes, and I was not happy about it, but she had already committed herself and I did not want to make a scene with her in front of INBOIL, so he would have something to tell his gang and they would all laugh.

That wouldn't make me feel good at all.

So we followed that drunken bum in what he said was only a quarter-of-a-mile, but it seèmed like a mile to me, weaving in and out, climbing higher and higher into the Piles.

"Nice day, isn't it?" INBOIL said, stopping to catch his breath by a large pile of what looked like cans, maybe.

"Yes, it is," Margaret said, smiling at INBOIL and pointing out a cloud that she particularly liked.

That really disgusted me: a decent woman· smiling at inBOIL. I could not help but wonder, what next?

Finally we arrived at that pile of stuff inBOIL thought was so great and had taken us so far into the Forgotten Works to see.

"Why, they're beautiful," Margaret said, smiling and went over and began putting them into her basket, the basket she had brought for such things.

I looked at them but they didn't show me anything. They were kind of ugly, if you want the truth. inBOIL leaned up against a forgotten thing that was just his size.

The Way Back

MARGARET AND I had a very long and quiet walk back to iDEATH.
I did not volunteer to carry her basket for her.

It was heavy and she was hot and sweaty and we had to stop
many times for her to rest.

We were sitting on a bridge. The bridge was made from
stones gathered at a distance and placed in their proper order.

"What's wrong?" she said. "What have I done?"

"Nothing's wrong. You've done nothing."

"Then why are you mad at me?"

"I'm not mad at you."

"Yes, you are."

"No, I'm not."

Something Is Going to Happen

THE NEXT MONTH it happened and no one knew what was coming. How could we imagine such a thing was going on in inBOIL's mind?

It had taken years to get over the tigers and the terrible things they had done to us. Why would anyone want to do something else? I don't know.

During the weeks before it happened everything went on as normal at iDEATH. I started working on another statue and Margaret kept going down to the Forgotten Works.

The statue did not go well and pretty soon I was only going down to iDEATH and staring at the statue. It just wasn't coming along which was nothing new for me. I had never had much luck at statues. I was thinking about getting a job down at the Watermelon Works.

Sometimes Margaret went down to the Forgotten Works by herself. It worried me. She was so pretty and inBOIL and that gang of his were so ugly. They might get ideas.

Why did she want to go down there all the time?

Rumors

TOWARD THE END of the month strange rumors began coming up from the Forgotten Works, rumors of violent denouncements of iDEATH by inBOIL.

There were rumors about him ranting and raving that iDEATH was all wrong the way we did it, and he knew how it should be done and then he said we handled the trout hatchery all wrong. It was a disgrace.

Imagine inBOIL saying anything about us, and there was a rumor about us being sissies and then something about the tigers that no one could understand.

Something about the tigers being a good deal.

I went down to the Forgotten Works with Margaret one afternoon. I didn't want to go down there, but I didn't want her to go down there alone either.

She wanted to get more things for her forgotten collection. She already had more things than were necessary.

She had filled her shack up and her room at iDEATH with these things. She even wanted to store some of them in my shack. I said NO.

I asked inBOIL what was up. He was drunk as usual, and his gang of bums was gathered around.

"You guys don't know anything about iDEATH. I'm going to

show you something about it soon. What real iDEATH is like," inBOIL said.

"You guys are a bunch of sissies. Only the tigers had any guts. I'm going to show you. We're going to show you all." He addressed this last thing to his gang. They cheered and held their bottles of whiskey up high, reaching toward the red sun.

The Way Back Again

"Why do you go down there?" I said.

"I just like forgotten things. I'm collecting them. I want a collection of them. I think they're cute. What's wrong with that?"

"What do you mean, what's wrong with that? Didn't you hear what that drunken bum said about us?"

"What does that have to do with forgotten things?" she said.

"They drink the stuff," I said.

Dinner That Night

DINNER THAT NIGHT was troubled at iDEATH. Everybody played with their food. Al had cooked up a mess of carrots. They were good, mixed with honey and spices, but nobody cared.

Everybody was worried about inBOIL. Pauline didn't touch her food. Neither did Charley. Strange thing, though: Margaret ate like a horse.

There had been a longish period of silence when Charley finally said, "I don't know what's going to happen. It looks serious. I've been afraid something like this was going to happen for a long time, ever since inBOIL got involved with the Forgotten Works, and took to making that whiskey of his, and getting men to go down there and live his kind of life.

"I've known something was going to happen. It's been due for a long time, and now it looks like it's here or will be shortly. Perhaps tomorrow. Who knows?"

"What are we going to do?" Pauline said. "What can we do?"

"Just wait," Charley said. "That's about all. We can't threaten them or defend ourselves until they've done something, and who knows what they are going to do. They won't tell us.

"I went down there myself yesterday morning, and I asked inBOIL what was up and he said, we'd see soon enough. They'd show us what iDEATH really was, none of the false stuff we have.

What do you know about this, Margaret? You've spent a lot of time down there lately."

Everybody looked at her.

"I don't know anything. I just get forgotten things down there. They don't tell me anything. They're always very nice to me."

Everybody tried hard not to look away from Margaret, but they couldn't help themselves, and looked away.

"We can take care of anything that happens," Fred said, breaking the silence. "Those drunken bums can't do anything we can't handle."

"You bet," Old Chuck said, though he was very old.

"You're right," Pauline said. "We can handle them. We live at iDEATH."

Margaret went right back to eating her carrots as if nothing had happened.

Pauline Again

I WAS VERY ANGRY with Margaret. She wanted to sleep with me at iDEATH, but I said, "NO, I want to go up to my shack and be alone."

She was very hurt by this and went off to the trout hatchery. I didn't care. Her performance at dinner had really disgusted me.

On my way out of iDEATH, I met Pauline in the living room. She was carrying a painting that she was going to put up on the wall.

"Hello," I said. "That's a lovely painting you have there. Did you paint that yourself?"

"Yes, I did."

"It looks very good."

The painting was of iDEATH a long time ago during one of its many changes. The painting looked like iDEATH used to look.

"I didn't know you painted," I said.

"Just in my spare time."

"It's really a nice painting."

"Thank you."

Pauline kind of blushed. I had never seen her blush before or perhaps I had not remembered so. It became her.

"You think everything is going to be all right, don't you?" she said, changing the subject.

"Yes," I said. "Don't worry."

Faces

I LEFT iDEATH and started up the road to my shack. It was suddenly a very cold night and the stars shone like ice. I wished I had brought my Mackinaw. I walked up the road until I saw the lanterns on the bridges.

They were the lanterns of a beautiful child and a trout on the real bridge, and the tiger lanterns on the abandoned bridge.

I could barely see the statue of somebody who had been killed by the tigers, but nobody knows who it was. So many were killed by the tigers until we killed the last tiger and burned its body at iDEATH and built the trout hatchery right over the spot.

The statue was standing in the river by the bridges. It looked sad as if it did not want to be a statue of somebody killed by the tigers a long time ago.

I stopped and stared at a distance. A little while passed and then I went to the bridge. I crossed through the dark tunnel of the covered real bridge, past the glowing faces, and up into the piney woods toward my shack.

Shack

I STOPPED ON THE BRIDGE to my shack. It felt good under my feet, made from all the things that I like, the things that suit me. I stared at my mother. She was only another shadow now against the night, but once she had been a good woman.

I went inside the shack and lit my lantern with a six-inch match. The watermelontrout oil burned with a beautiful light. It is a fine oil.

We mix watermelon sugar and trout juice and special herbs all together and in their proper time to make this fine oil that we use to light our world.

I was very sleepy but I didn't feel like sleeping. The sleepier I got, the less I felt like sleeping. I lay on my bed for a long time without taking off my clothes, and I left the lantern on and stared at the shadows in the room.

They were rather nice shadows for a time that was so ominous, that drew so near and all enclosing. I was so sleepy now that my eyes refused to close. The lids would not budge down. They were statues of eyes.

The Girl with the Lantern

AT LAST I couldn't stand lying there in bed any longer without sleeping. I went for one of my walks at night. I put on my red Mackinaw, so I wouldn't be cold. I guess it is this trouble that I have with sleeping that causes me to walk.

I went walking down by the aqueduct. That's a good place to walk. The aqueduct is about five miles long, but we don't know why because there is already water every place. There must be two or three hundred rivers here.

Charley himself hasn't the slightest idea why they built the aqueduct. "Maybe they were short of water a long time ago, and that's why they built the thing. I don't know. Don't ask me."

I once had a dream about the aqueduct being a musical instrument filled with water and bells hanging by small watermelon chains right at the top of the water and the water making the bells ring.

I told the dream to Fred and he said that it sounded all right to him. "That would really make beautiful music," he said.

I walked along the aqueduct for a while and then just stood there motionless for a long time where the aqueduct crosses the river by the Statue of Mirrors. I could see the light coming from all the tombs in the river down there. It's a favorite spot to be buried.

I climbed up a ladder on one of the columns and sat on the edge of the aqueduct, up about twenty feet, with my legs dangling over the edge.

I sat there for a long time without thinking about anything or noticing anything any more. I didn't want to. The night was passing with me sitting on the aqueduct.

Then I saw a lantern faraway and moving out of the piney woods. The lantern came down a road and then crossed over bridges and went through watermelon patches and stopped sometimes by the road, first this road and then that road.

I knew who the lantern belonged to. It was in the hand of a girl. I had seen her many times before walking at night, over the years.

But I had never seen the girl up close and I didn't know who she was. I knew she was sort of like me. Sometimes she had trouble sleeping at night.

It always comforted me when I saw her out there. I had never tried to find out who she was by going after her or even telling anyone about seeing her at night.

She was in a strange way mine and it comforted me to see her. I thought she was very pretty, but I didn't know what color hair she had.

Chickens

THE GIRL WITH THE LANTERN had left hours ago. I climbed down
from the aqueduct and stretched my legs. I walked back to
iDEATH in the dawn of a golden sun which would bring I knew
not what from inBOIL and that gang of his. We could only wait
and see.

The countryside was beginning to stir. I saw a farmer going
out to milk his cows. He waved when he saw me. He had on a
funny hat.

The roosters were beginning to crow. Their beak trumpets
travelled a loud and great distance. I arrived at iDEATH just be-
fore sunrise.

There were a couple of white chickens that had escaped from
a farmer someplace out in front of iDEATH pecking at the ground.
They looked at me and then they flew away. They were freshly
escaped. You could tell because their wings did not work like
real birds.

Bacon

AFTER A GOOD BREAKFAST of hot cakes and scrambled eggs and bacon, inBOIL and that gang of his arrived drunk at iDEATH, and it all began, then.

"This is really a good breakfast," Fred said to Pauline.

"Thank you."

Margaret was not there. I don't know where she was at. Pauline was there, though. She looked good, wearing a pretty dress.

Then we heard the front door bell ring. Old Chuck said he heard voices but it was impossible to hear voices from that distance.

"I'll get the door," Al said. He got up and left the kitchen and walked through the hall that led under the river to the living room.

"I wonder who it is," Charley said. I think Charley already knew who it was because he put down his fork and pushed his plate away.

Breakfast was over.

Al came back a few minutes later. He looked strange and worried. "It's inBOIL," he said. "He wants to see you, Charley. He wants to see all of us."

Now we all looked strange and worried.

We got up and went through the hall under the river and came out in the living room, right beside Pauline's painting. We went out on the front porch of iDEATH and there was inBOIL waiting, drunk.

Prelude

"YOU PEOPLE THINK you know about iDEATH. You don't know anything about iDEATH. You don't know anything about iDEATH," inBOIL said, and then there was wild laughter from that gang of his, who were just as drunk as he.

"Not a damn thing. You're all at a masquerade party," and then there was wild laughter from that gang of his.

"We're going to show you what iDEATH is really about," and then there was wild laughter.

"What do you know that we don't know?" Charley said.

"Let us show you. Let us into the trout hatchery and we'll show you a thing or two. Are you afraid to find out about iDEATH? What it really means? What a mockery you've made of it? All of you. And you, Charley, more than the rest of these clowns."

"Come, then," Charley said. "Show us iDEATH."

An Exchange

INBOIL and that gang of his staggered into iDEATH. "What a dump," one of them said. Their eyes were all red from that stuff they made and drank in such large quantities.

We crossed the metal bridge over the little river in the living room and went down the hall that leads to the trout hatchery.

One of INBOIL's gang was so drunk that he fell down and the others picked him up. They almost had to carry him along because he was so drunk. He kept saying over and over again, "When are we going to get to iDEATH?"

"You are at iDEATH."

"What is this?"

"iDEATH."

"Oh. When are we going to get to iDEATH?"

Margaret was nowhere around. I walked beside Pauline to kind of shield her from INBOIL and his trash. INBOIL saw her and came over. His overalls looked as if they had never been washed.

"Hi, Pauline," he said. "How are tricks?"

"You disgusting man," she replied.

INBOIL laughed.

"I'll mop the floor after you leave here," she said. "Wherever you walk is filth."

"Don't be that way," INBOIL said.

"How should I be?" Pauline said. "Look at you."

I had gone over to shield Pauline from inBOIL and now I almost had to step between them. Pauline was very mad. I had never seen Pauline mad before. She had quite a temper.

inBOIL laughed again and then he broke away from her and went up and joined Charley. Charley was not happy to see him either.

It was a strange procession travelling down the hall. "When are we going to get to iDEATH?"

The Trout Hatchery

THE TROUT HATCHERY at iDEATH was built years ago when the last tiger was killed and burned on the spot. We built the trout hatchery right there. The walls went up around the ashes.

The hatchery is small but designed with great care. The trays and ponds are made from watermelon sugar and stones gathered at a great distance and placed there in the order of that distance.

The water for the hatchery comes from the little river that joins up later with the main river in the living room. The sugar used is golden and blue.

There are two people buried at the bottom of the ponds in the hatchery. You look down past the young trout and see them lying there in their coffins, staring from beyond the glass doors. They wanted it that way, so they got it, being as they were keepers of the hatchery and at the same time, Charley's folks.

The hatchery has a beautiful tile floor with the tiles put together so gracefully that it's almost like music. It's a swell place to dance.

There is a statue of the last tiger in the hatchery. The tiger is on fire in the statue. We are all watching it.

inBOIL's iDEATH

"ALL RIGHT," Charley said. "Tell us about iDEATH. We're curious now about what you've been saying for years about us not knowing about iDEATH, about you knowing all the answers. Let's hear some of those answers."

"OK," inBOIL said. "This is what it's all about. You don't know what's really going on with iDEATH. The tigers knew more about iDEATH than you know. You killed all the tigers and burned the last one in here.

"That was all wrong. The tigers should never have been killed. The tigers were the true meaning of iDEATH. Without the tigers there could be no iDEATH, and you killed the tigers and so iDEATH went away, and you've lived here like a bunch of clucks ever since. I'm going to bring back iDEATH. We're all going to bring back iDEATH. My gang here and me. I've been thinking about it for years and now we're going to do it. iDEATH will be again."

inBOIL reached into his pocket and took out a jackknife.

"What are you going to do with that knife?" Charley said.

"I'll show you," inBOIL said. He pulled the blade out. It looked sharp. "This is iDEATH," he said, and took the knife and cut off his thumb and dropped it into a tray filled with trout just barely hatched. The blood started running down his hand and dripping on the floor.

Then all of inBOIL's gang took out jackknives and cut off their thumbs and dropped their thumbs here and there, in this tray, that pond until there were thumbs and blood all over the place.

The one who didn't know where he was said, "When do I cut off my thumb?"

"Right now," somebody said.

So he cut off his thumb, unevenly because he was so drunk. He did it in such a way that there was still part of the fingernail fastened to his hand.

"Why have you done this?" Charley said.

"It's only a beginning," inBOIL said. "This is what iDEATH should really look like."

"You all look silly," Charley said. "Without your thumbs."

"It's only a beginning," inBOIL said. "All right, men. Let's cut off our noses."

"Hail, iDEATH," they all shouted and cut off their noses. The one who was so drunk also put out his eye. They took their noses and dropped them all over the place.

One of them put his nose in Fred's hand. Fred took the nose and threw it in the guy's face.

Pauline did not act like a woman should under these circumstances. She was not afraid or made ill by this at all. She just kept getting madder and madder and madder. Her face was red with anger.

"All right, men. Off with your ears."

"Hail, iDEATH," and then there were ears all over the place and the trout hatchery was drowning in blood.

The one who was so drunk forgot that he had cut his right ear off already and was trying to cut it off again and was very confused because the ear wasn't there.

"Where's my ear?" he said. "I can't cut it off."

By now inBOIL and all his gang were bleeding to death. Some of them were already beginning to grow weak from the loss of blood and were sitting down on the floor.

inBOIL was STILL up and cutting fingers off his hands. "This is iDEATH," he said. "Oh, boy. This is really iDEATH." Finally he had to sit down, too, so he could bleed to death.

They were all on the floor now.

"I hope you think you've proved something," Charley said. "I don't think you've proved anything."

"We've proved iDEATH," inBOIL said.

Pauline suddenly started to leave the room. I went over to her, almost slipping on the blood and falling down.

"Are you all right?" I said, not knowing quite what to say. "Can I help you?"

"No," she said, on her way out. "I'm going to go get a mop and clean this mess up." When she said mess, she looked directly at inBOIL.

She left the hatchery and came back shortly with a mop. They were almost all dead now, except for inBOIL. He was still talking about iDEATH. "See, we've done it," he said.

Pauline started mopping up the blood and wringing it out into a bucket. When the bucket was almost full of blood, inBOIL died. "I am iDEATH," he said.

"You're an asshole," Pauline said.

And the last thing that inBOIL ever saw was Pauline standing beside him, wringing his blood out of the mop into the bucket.

Wheelbarrow

"WELL, that's that," Charley said.

INBOIL's sightless eyes stared at the statue of the tiger. There were many sightless eyes staring in the hatchery.

"Yeah," Fred said. "I wonder what it was all about."

"I don't know," Charley said. "I think they shouldn't have drunk that whiskey made from forgotten things. It was a mistake."

"Yeah."

We all joined Pauline in cleaning up the place, mopping up the blood and carting the bodies away. We used a wheelbarrow.

A Parade

"HERE, help me get this wheelbarrow down the stairs."

"There."

"Ah, thank you."

We piled the bodies out in front. No one knew quite what to do with them, except that we didn't want them in iDEATH any more.

A lot of people from the town had come up to see what was going on. There were maybe a hundred people there by the time we got the last body wheeled out.

"What happened?" the schoolteacher said.

"They made a mess out of themselves," Old Chuck said.

"Where are their thumbs and features?" Doc Edwards asked.

"Right over there in that bucket," Old Chuck said. "They cut them off with their jackknives. We don't know why."

"What are we going to do with the bodies?" Fred said. "We're not going to put them in tombs, are we?"

"No," Charley said. "We have to do something else."

"Take them to their shacks at the Forgotten Works," Pauline said. "Burn them. Burn their shacks. Burn them together and then forget them."

"That's a good idea," Charley said. "Let's get some wagons and take them down there. What a terrible thing."

We put the bodies in the wagons. By then almost everybody in watermelon sugar had gathered at iDEATH. We all started down to the Forgotten Works together.

We started off very slowly. We looked like a parade barely moving toward YOU MIGHT GET LOST. I walked beside Pauline.

Bluebells

THERE WAS a warm golden sun shining down on us and on the slowly nearing Piles of the Forgotten Works. We crossed rivers and bridges and walked beside farms, meadows and through the piney woods and by fields of watermelons.

The piles of the Forgotten works were like chunks of half-mountains and half-apparatus that glowed like gold.

An almost festive spirit was coming now from the crowd. They were relieved that inBOIL and that gang of his were dead.

Children began picking flowers along the way and pretty soon there were many flowers in the parade, so that it became a kind of vase filled with roses and daffodils and poppies and bluebells.

"It's over," Pauline said, and then, turning, she threw her arms around me and gave me a very friendly hug to prove that it was all over. I felt her body against me.

Margaret Again, Again, Again, Again

INBOIL and the bodies of his gang were put into a shack and drenched with watermelontrout oil. We brought along a barrelful for that purpose and then all the other shacks were drenched with watermelontrout oil.

All the people stood back and just as Charley was getting ready to set fire to the shack where the bodies were, Margaret came waltzing out of the Forgotten Works.

"What's up?" she said. She acted as if nothing had happened, as if we were all down there on some kind of picnic.

"Where have you been?" Charley said, looking a little bewildered at Margaret, who was as cool as a cucumber.

"In the Forgotten Works," she said. "I came down here early this morning, before sunrise, to look for things. What's wrong? Why are you all down here at the Forgotten Works?"

"Don't you know what happened?" Charley said.

"No," she said.

"Did you see INBOIL when you came down here this morning?"

"No," she said. "They were all asleep. What's wrong?" She looked all around. "Where's INBOIL?"

"I don't even know if I can tell you," Charley said. "He's dead and all his gang, too."

"Dead. You must be joking."

"Why? No, they came up to iDEATH a couple of hours ago and they all killed themselves in the trout hatchery. We've brought their bodies down here to burn them. They made a terrible scene."

"I don't believe it," Margaret said. "I just can't believe it. What kind of joke is this?"

"It's no joke," Charley said.

Margaret looked around. She could see that almost everybody was there. She saw me standing beside Pauline and she ran over to me and said, "Is it true?"

"Yes."

"Why?"

"I don't know. None of us do. They just came up to iDEATH and killed themselves. It's a mystery to us."

"Oh no," Margaret said. "How did they do it?"

"With jackknives."

"Oh, no," Margaret said. She was very shocked, dazed. She grabbed ahold of my hand.

"This morning?" she said, almost to no one now.

"Yes."

Her hand felt cold and awkward in my hand as if the fingers were too small to fit. I could only stare at her who had disappeared into the Forgotten Works that morning.

Shack Fever

CHARLEY TOOK a six-inch match and set fire to the shack that contained inBOIL and the bodies of his gang. We all stood back and the flames went up higher and higher and burned with that beautiful light that watermelontrout oil makes.

Then Charley set fire to the other shacks and they burned just as brightly, and pretty soon the heat was so bad that we had to stand farther and farther back until we were in the fields.

We watched for an hour or so and the shacks were fairly gone by then. Charley stood there watching very quietly. inBOIL had once been his brother.

Some of the children were playing in the fields. They got tired of watching the fire. It had been very exciting at first, but then the children grew tired of it and decided to do something else.

Pauline sat down on the grass. The flames brought total peace to her face. She looked as if she had just been born.

I stopped holding Margaret's hand and she was still in a daze over what was happening. She sat by herself in the grass, holding her hands together as if they were dead.

As the flames diminished to very little, a strong wind came out of the Forgotten Works and scattered ashes rapidly through the air. After while Fred yawned, I dreamt.

Book Three:
Margaret

Job

I woke up feeling refreshed and stared at my watermelon ceiling, how nice it looked, before getting out of bed. I wondered what time it was. I was supposed to meet Fred for lunch at the cafe in town.

I got up and went outside and stretched again on the front porch of my shack, feeling the cool stones under my bare feet, feeling their distance. I looked at the gray sun.

The river shone not quite lunch time yet, so I went over to the river and got some water and threw it in my face to finish the job of waking up.

Meat Loaf

I MET Fred at the cafe. He was already there, waiting for me. Doc Edwards was with him. Fred was looking at the menu.

"Hello," I said.

"Hi."

"Hello," Doc Edwards said.

"You were really in a hurry this morning," I said. "You looked like you needed a horse."

"That's right. I had to go deliver a baby. A litle girl joined us this morning."

"That's fine," I said. "Who's the lucky father?"

"Do you know Ron?"

"Yeah. He lives in that shack by the shoeshop. Right?"

"Yeah. That's Ron. He's got a fine little girl."

"You were really moving along. I didn't know you had that much speed left in you."

"Yes. Yes."

"How are you, Fred?" I said.

"Fine. I put in a good morning's work. What did you do?"

"Planted a few flowers."

"Did you work on your book?"

"No, I planted a few flowers and took a long nap."

"Lazyhead."

"By the way," Doc Edwards said. "How's that book coming along?"

"Oh, it's coming along."

"Fine. What's it about?"

"Just what I'm writing down: one word after another."

"Good."

The waitress came over and asked us what we were having for lunch. "What are you boys having for lunch?" she said. She had been the waitress there for years. She had been a young girl there and now she was not young any more.

"Today's special is meat loaf, isn't it?" Doc Edwards said.

"Yes, 'Meat loaf for a gray day is the best way,' that's our motto," she said.

Everybody laughed. It was a good joke.

"I'll have some meat loaf," Fred said.

"What about you?" the waitress said. "Meat loaf?"

"Yeah, meat loaf," I said.

"Three meat loaves," the waitress said.

Apple Pie

AFTER LUNCH Doc Edwards had to leave early to go and check on Ron's woman and the new baby to see that they were doing all right.

"See you later," he said.

Fred and I stayed there for a while and drank another cup of coffee at our leisure. Fred put two lumps of watermelon sugar in his coffee.

"How's Margaret doing?" he said. "Have you seen her or heard from her?"

"No," I said. "I told you that this morning."

"She's in pretty bad shape over you and Pauline," Fred said. "She's having a lot of trouble accepting it. I was talking to her brother yesterday. He said she's got a broken heart."

"I can't help that," I said.

"Why are you mad at her?" Fred said. "You don't think she had anything to do with iNBOIL just because everybody else does, except Pauline and me?

"There's no proof. It doesn't even make sense in the first place. It was just a coincidence that linked them together. You don't believe she had anything to do with iNBOIL, do you?"

"I don't know," I said.

Fred shrugged his shoulders and took a sip of his coffee. The waitress came over and asked us if we wanted a piece of pie for dessert. "We've got some apple pie that really tastes good," she said.

"I'd like a piece of pie," Fred said.

"What about you?"

"No," I said.

Literature

"WELL, I've got to get back to work," Fred said. "The plank press calls. What are you going to do?"

"I think I'll go write," I said. "Work on my book for a while."

"That sounds ambitious," Fred said. "Is the book about weather like the schoolteacher said?"

"No, it's not about weather."

"Good," Fred said. "I wouldn't want to read a book about weather."

"Have you ever read a book?" I said.

"No," Fred said. "I haven't but I don't think I'd want to start by reading one about clouds."

The Way

FRED WENT OFF to the Watermelon Works and I started back to my shack to write, and then I decided not to. I didn't know what to do.

I could go back to iDEATH and talk to Charley about an idea I had or I could go find Pauline and make love to her or I could go to the Statue of Mirrors and sit down there for a while.

That's what I did.

The Statue of Mirrors

EVERYTHING IS REFLECTED in the Statue of Mirrors if you stand there long enough and empty your mind of everything else but the mirrors, and you must be careful not to want anything from the mirrors. They just have to happen.

An hour or so passed as my mind drained out. Some people cannot see anything in the Statue of Mirrors, not even themselves.

Then I could see iDEATH and the town and the Forgotten Works and rivers and fields and the piney woods and the ball park and the Watermelon Works.

I saw Old Chuck on the front porch of iDEATH. He was scratching his head and Charley was in the kitchen buttering himself a slice of toast.

Doc Edwards was walking down the street from Ron's shack and a dog was following behind him, sniffing his footsteps. The dog stopped at one particular footstep and stood there with its tail wagging above the footstep. The dog really liked that one.

The shacks of inBOIL and that gang of his lay now only as ashes by the gate to the Forgotten Works. A bird was looking near the ashes for something. The bird didn't find what it was looking for, got tired and flew away.

I saw Pauline walking through the piney woods up toward

my shack. She was carrying a painting with her. It was a surprise for me.

I saw some kids playing baseball in the ball park. One of the kids pitching had a good fast ball and a lot of control. He threw five strikes in a row.

I saw Fred directing his crew in the making of a golden plank of watermelon sugar. He was telling somebody to be careful with his end.

I saw Margaret climbing an apple tree beside her shack. She was crying and had a scarf knotted around her neck. She took the loose end of the scarf and tied it to a branch covered with young apples. She stepped off the branch and then she was standing by herself on the air.

The Grand Old Trout Again

I STOPPED LOOKING into the Statue of Mirrors. I'd seen enough for that day. I sat down on a couch by the river and stared into the water of the deep pool that's there. Margaret was dead.

There was a swirl of water on the surface that cleared the pool all the way down to the bottom, and I saw The Grand Old Trout staring back at me, with the little iDEATH bell hanging from his jaw.

He must have swum upstream from where they were putting the tomb in. That's a long way for an old trout. He must have left just after I did.

The Grand Old Trout did not take his eyes off me. He remained stationary in the water, staring intently at me as he had been doing earlier in the day when he lay by the tomb they were putting in.

There was another swirl of water on the surface of the pool and then I could not see The Grand Old Trout any more. When the pool cleared again, The Grand Old Trout was gone. I stared at the place where he had been in the river. It was empty now like a room.

Getting Fred

I WENT DOWN to the Watermelon Works to see Fred. He was rather surprised to see me down there for the second time that day.

"Hi," he said, looking up from a golden plank that he had been checking out for something. "What's up?"

"It's Margaret," I said.

"Have you seen her?"

"Yes."

"What happened?"

"She's dead. I saw her in the Statue of Mirrors. She hanged herself from an apple tree with her blue scarf."

Fred put the plank down. He bit his lip and ran his hand through his hair. "When did this happen?"

"Just a little while ago. Nobody knows she's dead yet."

Fred shook his head. "I guess we'd better go get her brother."

"Where's he at?"

"He's helping a farmer put a new roof on his barn. We'll go there."

Fred told the crew to knock off for the day. They were quite pleased when Fred told them this. "Thanks, boss," they said.

We left the Watermelon Works with Fred suddenly looking very tired.

The Wind Again

THE GRAY SUN shone feebly. A wind came up and things that could rustle or move in the wind did so all about us as we walked down the road to the barn.

"Why do you think she killed herself?" Fred said. "Why should she do a thing like that? She was so young. So young."

"I don't know," I said. "I don't know why she killed herself."

"It's just terrible," Fred said. "I wish I didn't have to think about it. You haven't the slightest idea, huh? You haven't seen her?"

"No, I was looking into the Statue of Mirrors and she hanged herself there. She's dead now."

Margaret's Brother

MARGARET'S BROTHER was up on the barn roof, nailing blue watermelon shingles down and the farmer was climbing up the ladder, bringing him another bundle of shingles.

Her brother saw us coming up the road and stood up on the barn roof and waved at quite a distance before we got there.

"I don't like this," Fred said.

"Hello, there," her brother yelled.

"What brings you up this way?" the farmer yelled.

We waved back but didn't say anything until we got there.

"Howdy," the farmer said, shaking hands with us. "What are you doing up this way?"

Margaret's brother climbed down the ladder. "Hello," he said and shook our hands and stood there waiting for us to say something. We were strangely quiet and they picked up on it immediately.

Fred pawed at the ground with his boot. He drew a kind of half-circle with his right boot on the ground, and then he erased it with his left boot. This took only a few seconds.

"What's wrong?" the farmer said.

"Yeah, what's wrong?" her brother said.

"It's Margaret," Fred said.

"What's wrong with Margaret?" her brother said. "Tell me."

117

"She's dead," Fred said.

"How did it happen?"

"She hanged herself."

Margaret's brother stared straight ahead for a little while. His eyes were dim. Nobody said anything. Fred drew another circle in the dust, and then kicked it away.

"It's for the best," Margaret's brother said, finally. "Nobody's to blame. She had a broken heart."

The Wind Again, Again

WE WENT and got the body. The farmer had to stay behind.
He said he would have come along but he had to stay and milk
his cows. The wind was blowing harder now and a few small
things fell down.

Necklace

MARGARET'S BODY was hanging from the apple tree in front of her shack and blowing in the wind. Her neck was at a wrong angle and her face was the color of what we learn to know as death.

Fred climbed up the tree and cut the scarf with his jackknife while Margaret's brother and I lowered her body gently down. He took her body then, and carried it into the shack and lay it down upon the bed.

We stood there.

"Let's take her to iDEATH," Fred said. "That's where she belongs."

Her brother looked relieved for the first time since we had told him of her death.

He went to a large chest by the window and took out a necklace that had small metal trout encircling it. He lifted up her head and fastened the clasp of the necklace. He brushed Margaret's hair out of her eyes.

Then he wrapped her body in a bedspread that had iDEATH crocheted upon it in one of its many and lasting forms. One of her feet was sticking out. The toes looked cold and gently at rest.

120

Couch

WE TOOK Margaret back to iDEATH. Somehow everybody there had already heard of her death and they were waiting for us. They were out on the front porch.

Pauline ran down the stairs to me. She was very upset and her cheeks were wet with tears. "Why?" she said. "Why?"

I put my arm around her the best I could. "I don't know," I said.

Margaret's brother carried her body up the stairs into iDEATH. Charley opened the door for him. "Here, let me open the door for you."

"Thank you," her brother said. "Where shall I put her?"

"On the couch back in the trout hatchery," Charley said. "That's where we put our dead."

"I don't remember the way," her brother said. "I haven't been here for a long time."

"I'll show you. Follow me," Charley said.

"Thank you."

They went off to the trout hatchery. Fred went with them and so did Old Chuck and Al and Bill. I stayed behind with my arm around Pauline. She was still crying. I guess she really liked Margaret.

Tomorrow

PAULINE AND I went down for a walk by the river in the living room. It was now nearing sundown. Tomorrow the sun would be black, soundless. The night would continue but the stars would not shine and it would be warm like day and everything would be without sound.

"This is horrible," Pauline said. "I feel so bad. Why did she kill herself? Was it my fault for loving you?"

"No," I said. "It was nobody's fault. Just one of those things."

"We were such good friends. We were like sisters. I'd hate to think it was my fault."

"Don't," I said.

Carrots

DINNER THAT NIGHT was a quiet affair at iDEATH. Margaret's brother stayed and had dinner with us. Charley invited him.

Al cooked up a mess of carrots again. He broiled them with mushrooms and a sauce made from watermelon sugar and spices. There was hot bread fresh from the oven and sweet butter and glasses of ice-cold milk.

About halfway through dinner, Fred started to say something that looked as if it were important, but then he changed his mind and went back to eating his carrots.

Margaret's Room

AFTER DINNER everybody went into the living room and it was decided to hold the funeral tomorrow morning, even though it would be dark and there would be no sound and everything would have to be done in silence.

"If it's all right with you," Charley said to Margaret's brother. "She'll be buried in that tomb we've been working on. They finished it this afternoon."

"That would be perfect," her brother said.

"It will be dark and there will be no sound, but I think we can take care of everything."

"Yeah," her brother said.

"Fred, will you go and tell the people in the town about the funeral? Some of them might want to go. Also alert the Tomb Crew about the funeral. And see if you can find some flowers."

"Sure, Charley. I'll take care of it."

"It's our custom to brick up the rooms of those who lived here when they die," Charley said.

"What does that mean?" Margaret's brother said.

"We put bricks across the door and close the room forever."

"That sounds all right."

Bricks

PAULINE AND Margaret's brother and Charley and Bill, he had the bricks, and I went to Margaret's room. Charley opened the door.

Pauline was carrying a lantern. She put it down on Margaret's table and lit the lantern that was there with a long watermelon match.

There were now two lights.

The room was filled with things from the Forgotten Works. Every place you looked there was something forgotten that was piled on another forgotten thing.

Charley shook his head. "A lot of forgotten things in here. We don't even know what most of the things are," he said to nobody.

Margaret's brother sighed.

"Is there anything you want to take with you?" Charley said.

Her brother looked all around the room very carefully and very sadly and then shook his head, too. "No, brick it all up."

We stepped outside and Bill started putting the bricks in place. We watched for a little while. There were tears in Pauline's eyes.

"Please spend the night with us," Charley said.

"Thank you," Margaret's brother said.

"I'll show you to your room. Good night," Charley said to us. He went off with her brother. He was saying something to him.

"Let's go, Pauline," I said.

"All right, honey."

"I think you'd better sleep with me tonight."

"Yes," she said.

We left Bill putting the bricks in place. They were watermelon bricks made from black, soundless sugar. They made no sound as he worked with them. They would seal off the forgotten things forever.

My Room

PAULINE AND I went to my room. We took off our clothes and got into bed. She took off her clothes first and I watched.

"Are you going to blow the lantern out?" she said, leaning forward as I got into bed last.

She did not have any covers up over her breasts. The nipples were hard. They were almost the same color as her lips. They looked beautiful in the lantern light. Her eyes were red from crying. She looked very tired.

"No," I said.

She put her head back on the pillow and smiled ever so faintly. Her smile was like the color of her nipples.

"No," I said.

The Girl with the Lantern Again

AFTER WHILE I let Pauline go to sleep, but then I had my usual trouble sleeping. She was warm and sweet-smelling beside me. Her body called me to sleep as if it were a band of trumpets. I lay there for a long time before I got up and went for one of the walks I take at night.

I stood there with my clothes on, watching Pauline sleep. Strange, how well Pauline has slept since we have been going steady together, for Pauline was the girl who went for the long walks at night, carrying the lantern. Pauline was the girl I wondered so much about, walking up and down the roads, stopping at this place, this bridge, this river, these trees in the piney woods.

Her hair is blonde and now she is asleep.

After we started going steady she stopped her long walks at night, but I still continue mine. It suits me to take these long walks at night.

Margaret Again, Again, Again, Again, Again

I WENT TO THE TROUT HATCHERY and stood there staring at the cold undelightful body now of Margaret. She lay upon the couch and there were lanterns all around. The trout had trouble sleeping.

There were some fingerlings darting around in a tray that had a lantern by the edge of it, illuminating Margaret's face. I stared at the fingerlings for a long time, hours passed, until they went to sleep. They were now like Margaret.

Good Ham

WE WOKE UP an hour or so before sunrise and had an early breakfast. When the sun came up over the edge of our world, the darkness would continue and there would be no sound today. Our voices would be gone. If you dropped something, there would be no sound. The rivers would be silent.

"It's going to be a long day," Pauline said, as she put on her dress, pulling it over her long smooth neck.

We had ham and eggs, hashbrowns and toast. Pauline cooked breakfast and I offered to help her. "Is there anything I can do?" I said.

"No," she said. "I've got everything under control but thanks for the offer."

"You're welcome."

We all had breakfast together, including Margaret's brother. He sat next to Charley.

"This is good ham," Fred said.

"We'll hold the funeral later on in the morning," Charley said. "Everybody knows what they have to do and we can write notes if anything out of the ordinary comes up. We just have a few moments of sound left."

"Ummmm—good ham," Fred said.

Sunrise

PAULINE AND I were in the kitchen talking when the sun came up. She was washing the dishes and I was drying them. I was drying a frying pan and she was washing the coffee cups.

"I feel a little bit better today," she said.

"Good," I said.

"How did I sleep last night?"

"Like a top."

"I had a bad dream. I hope I didn't wake you up."

"No."

"The shock yesterday was something. I don't know. I just didn't expect things to turn out this way, but they have, and I guess there's nothing we can do about it."

"That's right," I said. "Just take things the way they happen."

Pauline turned toward me and said, "I guess the funeral will—"

Escutcheon

MARGARET WAS DRESSED in death robes made from watermelon sugar and adorned with beads of foxfire, so that the light would shine forever from her tomb at night and on the black, soundless days. This one.

She had been prepared now for the tomb. We moved in lanterns and silence about iDEATH, waiting for the townspeople to come.

They came. Thirty or forty arrived, including the editor of the newspaper. It is published once a year. The schoolteacher and Doc Edwards were there and then we started the funeral.

Margaret was carried on the Escutcheon we use for the dead, made from pine ornamented with glass and little distant stones.

Everybody had torches and lanterns and we carried her body out of the trout hatchery and through the living room and out the door and across the porch and down the steps of iDEATH.

Sunny Morning

THE PROCESSION moved slowly and in total silence down the road to the new tomb that now belonged to Margaret, the one I had watched them building yesterday, putting the finishing touches on for Margaret. It was getting warm as the sun climbed higher in the sky. There was not even the sound of our footsteps or anything.

The Tomb Crew

THE TOMB CREW was waiting for us. They still had the Shaft in place and they started the pump going when they saw us coming.

We turned the body over to them and they went about putting it in the tomb. They've had a lot of experience doing that. They carried her body down the Shaft and put it in the tomb. They closed the glass door and started to seal it up.

Pauline, Charley, Fred, Old Chuck and I stood there together in a little group and watched them. Pauline took my arm. Margaret's brother came over and joined us.

After the Tomb Crew had sealed the door, they turned the pump off and removed the hose from the Shaft.

Then they harnessed up some horses with ropes to the two pulleys that were hanging from the Shaft Gallows. Ropes went from the Shaft Gallows to hooks in the Shaft itself.

That's how they get the Shaft out.

The horses strained forward and the Shaft was pulled free from the bottom of the river and was lifted up onto the shore and was now half-hanging from the Shaft Gallows.

The Tomb Crew and their horses looked tired. Everything was done in total silence. Not a sound came from the horses or the men or the Shaft or the river or the people watching.

We saw the light shining up from Margaret, the light that

came from the foxfire upon her robes. We took flowers and threw them upstream above her tomb.

The flowers drifted down over the light coming from her: roses and daffodils and poppies and bluebells floated on by.

The Dance

IT IS A CUSTOM HERE to hold a dance in the trout hatchery after a funeral. Everybody comes and there's a good band and much dancing goes on. We all like to waltz.

After the funeral we went back to iDEATH and prepared for the dance. Party decorations were put up in the hatchery and refreshments were prepared for the dance.

Everybody got ready in silence. Charley put on some new overalls. Fred spent half an hour combing his hair and Pauline put on high heel shoes.

We could not start the party until there was sound, so that the musical instruments would work and we could work with them in our own style, mostly waltzing.

Cooks Together

PAULINE AND Al together cooked an early dinner that we had late in the afternoon. It was very hot outside, so they prepared something light. They made a potato salad that somehow ended up having a lot of carrots in it.

Their Instruments Playing

PEOPLE FROM THE TOWN began arriving for the dance about half an hour before sundown. We took their Mackinaws and hats and showed them into the trout hatchery.

Everybody seemed to be in fairly good spirits. The musicians took out their instruments and waited for the sun to go down.

It would only be a few moments now. We all waited patiently. The room glowed with lanterns. The trout swam back and forth in their trays and ponds. We would dance around them.

Pauline looked very pretty. Charley's new overalls looked good. I don't know why Fred's hair looked as if he hadn't combed it at all.

The musicians were poised with their instruments. They were ready to go. It would only be a few seconds now, I wrote.

This novel was started May 13, 1964 in a house at Bolinas, California, and was finished July 19, 1964 in the front room at 123 Beaver Street, San Francisco, California. This novel is for Don Allen, Joanne Kyger and Michael McClure.

Richard Brautigan was born January 30, 1935, in the Pacific North-west. He was the author of ten novels, nine volumes of poetry, and a collection of short stories. He lived for many years in San Francisco, and toward the end of his life he divided his time between a ranch in Montana and Tokyo. Brautigan was a literary idol of the 1960s and early 1970s whose comic genius and iconoclastic vision of American life caught the imagination of young people everywhere. Brautigan came of age during the Haight-Ashbury period and has been called "the last of the Beats." His early books became required reading for the hip generation, and Trout Fishing in America *sold two million copies throughout the world. Brautigan was a god of the counterculture, a phenomenon who saw his star rise to fame and fortune, only to plummet during the next decade. Driven to drink and despair, he committed suicide in Bolinas, California, at the age of forty-nine.*